VOICES OF THE SOUTH

COME BACK, LOLLY RAY

COME BACK,

LOLLY RAY

Beverly Lowry

LOUISIANA STATE UNIVERSITY PRESS
BATON ROUGE   MM

Copyright © 1976, 1977 by Beverly Lowry
Originally published by Doubleday & Company, Inc.
LSU Press edition published 2000 by arrangement with the author
All rights reserved
Manufactured in the United States of America

09 08 07 06 05 04 03 02 01 00
5 4 3 2 1

Library of Congress Cataloging-in-Publication Data

Lowry, Beverly.
    Come back, Lolly Ray / Beverly Lowry.
        p. cm. – (Voices of the South)
    ISBN 0-8071-2574-1 (alk. paper)
    1. Southern States–Fiction. I. Title. II. Series

    PS3562.O92 C66 2000
    813'.54–dc21

                                                     99-086603

Come Back, Lolly Ray first appeared in condensed form in *Redbook*.

The paper in this book meets the guidelines for permanence and durability of the
Committee on Production Guidelines for Book Longevity of the Council on
Library Resources. ∞

For Glenn

I

LOLLY

The sun and river were to the west, back over their shoulders on the other side of the levee. The main street of town —along which they waited, impatiently—dead-ended there, at the foot of the levee. Holding on to one another for support, they leaned out over the curb to see if she was coming yet and some even stepped into the street and stood hands cupped over their eyes in the middle of it, looking for a sign of her . . . until someone else shouted for them to get themselves back up on the sidewalk where everybody else was. Children, hot, played chase in and out of their parents' legs and pulled at their clothes and, wanting to get on with what they came for, gave notice if she wasn't here soon they were going home. Though by the calendar autumn had arrived, the day was still and hot, and no breeze at all came to dilute the heat pouring thick and heavy down on them. Even now, late afternoon, the sun persisted. Low, resting on the levee's crest like a sleeping baby's head, it seemed to want to see her too, and refused to sink behind. There was no sign yet of the north wind predicted to blow in that day and cool things off.

She wore a gold suit. Because the music was too far behind her, they would not hear it first, but awaited another clear and familiar signal. When the sun's light butted headlong into the bright gold thing she wore and was reflected off it: that quick flash of light. They watched for it. And just about the time the kids' squirming started turning into fistfights, the word passed that it had happened, the light had flashed and she was coming; she was on her way. Children screamed and pushed at each other for places to see from. The adults did not scream, but pushed. They couldn't see her distinctly at first because of the light bouncing back and forth. When she turned the corner at Hawthorne and came down Main toward them, all they could make out was a waving gold flash moving alone down the center of the street, boldly into the sun; as hot and bright as it was, braving it; coming down Main toward them and the river, directly into the Friday afternoon sun. The backs of their necks dripped with sweat as they kept their heads turned toward her.

At her middle, there were, in addition to the sun's reflection and her dazzling gold suit, yet two other bright things but these were silver, and moving. And when one of them went suddenly up to her face then past her head, people leaned out even farther and did what they could to help themselves see: they made awnings of their hands, or put spread fingers palm-out in front of their eyes, peering between them as if through blinds. The children pointed as the silver thing went farther and farther up over her, and screamed as it held there, a gleaming disc of silver which

soon became pulled out into a starlike shape by the light of
the sun. Heat waves rose up around her ankles and her body
swam and turned under the silver star, like a goldfish in a
pool of heat. Then as the silver started to come down, they
held their breaths and followed it, waiting to see if it hit the
street, wondering if it would, hoping it would, at the same
time believing it would not, caught up in the excitement of
both possibilities. Either way, they would have the exhilaration they came for. Then when it did not hit, when she
stopped it at her waist where the other one was and moved
them both one after the other quickly in succession behind
her, around her, under her leg, around her neck, and finally
back up over her so high the tallest old oaks lining Main
could not with their topmost branches reach it, then the
people released their breaths, sighed, clapped proudly,
pounded their children on their backs, and said among
themselves, "That Lolly . . . that girl! She never misses!"

She was their twirler, both in her time and after it, *the*
town twirler, a title she could claim as surely as if she had
been crowned, no matter who else was twirling while she
was or continued to after she was through, because Lolly
Ray Lasswell's name and legend would be passed on from
generation to generation as the town of Eunola's own. Like
Graham, the town drunk, like Booth Oates, the town idiot,
and Alberta, the town whore, and even, though he was long
gone, Sexton Cunningham, Eunola's comical and self-styled
historical figure, Lolly would not be deposed by time, as
they had not, the tales of their accomplishment now having
been established outside time and ordinary human considerations. By the time Lolly was twirling, Sexton had been
dead fifty-six years and Graham, seven. But Graham was
still the town drunk, even though people in Eunola were a

drinking community, and except for the hard-shelled Baptist
refugees from Texas and the hills (those who always seemed
to be squinting, sun or no, who waited Fridays not for Lolly
but the band behind her), everybody thought it was all right
to do it and most did. But there was not and had never been
as far back as anybody could remember a drunk like Graham, who was above every other consideration in his life a
drunk, who never merely *drank* but shaped his drinking as if
it were an art: until it was his life itself. His capacities were
sublime; his legend established; his place, unshakable. Because he transcended ordinary notions of ordinary limita-
tions, he was exalted, and Lolly was no different from Graham. She was that kind of twirler.

As she got closer to the big crowd (which gathered about
halfway up Main toward the levee because the big front-
porched houses down toward Hawthorne and the railroad
tracks were Eunola's oldest, and their inhabitants, also Eunola's oldest, prized their roses and camellias and didn't care
for parade watchers trampling up the Bermuda grass), and
they could see her better, their excitement grew. They became quieter, concentrating strictly on her now, unwilling
to risk even a glance away in the chance it might be the
moment when she did a special trick or, as noteworthy,
dropped her baton. The promise of either kept them on
edge, anticipating. She was shining now, coming closer, like
a piece of the sun. Her uniform was made entirely of dime-
sized solid gold overlapping sequins, each of which was
attached at the top only so that when she moved the sequins
shifted and swung a split second later and it looked as
though either she was moving twice every time or that
the uniform as it caught the sun and gave it back to them
was moving on its own. It was a one-piece, sleeveless, legless

costume, designed and made by Lolly herself, elasticized as
far as it went, which in length was just far enough that arcs
of her butt slipped out when she high-stepped. Her boots
were silver up to her knees, tight, zippered, with two-inch
heels and three gold tassels in a row swinging down the
front. She was tiny, and thin. Her skin was pale; her hair the
color of deep wet mud with an overlay of rust, glittering as
the river was now with the sun almost in it, bouncing on her
shoulders as if it had springs. As the band was still not in
sight, she came alone, prancing by herself, though the sound
of drums could now be heard approaching.

As she neared the last of the oak trees before the commer-
cial part of downtown, the crowd, having waited so long,
grew edgier. Children's screams thinned to squeals. They
could see her face. People said . . . especially majorettes
and majorettes' mothers . . . she was not *pretty*, not really.
She was too pale, too thin, her features too large for the size
of her face. And her nose . . . ! (Majorettes doted on the
shape and length of Lolly's nose, which instead of turning
up in the popular fashion, pointed down.) Curls of her thick
coarse hair draped heavily about her face and half-covered
her eyes, which, cool and blue, focused on something her
fans could never determine the exact location or nature of.
Certainly she never looked at them. Just like her daddy,
some said. Never gives anybody the time of day unless he's
pinned down and asked it.

She had two batons, which she turned like wheels in front
of her, her arms straight out. Suddenly, about half a
block from where they waited, she slapped them one over
each arm and pranced straight ahead in a kind of goosestep,
her arms in absolute and unshakable rhythm with her feet.
As one baton went straight up beside her head, the other

reached its position alongside her thigh. Alternating. Up
. . . thigh, arm, baton . . . down. Locked in. Up . . . catching the sun again and again.

In the middle of the intersection just before the crowd's
edge she stopped dead still, square in the center under
the traffic light which blinked on and off, red, for the
parade. Each thing she did was absolutely distinct from the
next so that if afterward you had been asked you could have
said she did this-then-this-then-this in clear succession with
no overlap. She raised both arms, batons east-west, perpendicular to her arms, and pointed one toe toward the levee
and one back toward the railroad tracks. Keeping her knees
stiff and her head straight, her chin out toward the sun, she
started easing her way down, sliding into a full split. And
very slowly the batons began to turn in time with her
sliding. The closer she got to the street, the faster the
batons turned, until, when the tops of her thighs were
within the heat of the concrete and she had thrown her
head back, her eyes were facing the blinking light above,
the tips of her hair were grazing her butt and the batons
were speeding like crazy. She looked up . . . at the batons?
The light? The sky? They wondered but could not tell. People in back leaned down on shoulders in front of them to see
her going down and to try to figure out what it was she saw,
for Lolly never gave them everything they came for. As natural a dream as those that come in sleep, she let them grope
for their own endings and explanations and slid on down
then as easily as if on slick glass and when she was all the
way down sat as if it were natural to be split apart one leg
due east and one due west, naked against the hot street, facing the awful sun, toes pointed hard as street signs, her head
still tilted.

On the sidewalk a little girl marched like Lolly's shadow, turning a circus baton in imitation. She, too, was on the concrete with her legs spread and as Lolly hopped gracefully back up on her feet and started off again, the little girl struggled to her feet. Unlike Lolly, the child acknowledged the applause and cheers. Lolly's eyes, still abstracted, disregarded them. But she did smile. Her teeth were large and straight, and with her head back shining, the smile held out promises.

About that time the band turned from Hawthorne down Main and the gaunt women in plain belted dresses, the teetotaling Baptists who had not looked at Lolly, or if they had, had looked quickly away as if it were sinful, clapped one hand stiffly against the other in recognition of the band's approach.

The line of majorettes across the front of the band (and no one referred to Lolly as a majorette except the majorettes themselves, who said the only difference between them was that Lolly wore a different uniform and could do a few more tricks) in their heavy chin-strapped, plumed tin soldier hats and standard white majorette boots and mid-thigh satin uniforms came red-faced into the threatening sun, marching as instructed, knee up groin high, toe pointed, to the music, keeping the line straight, and when the people got around to turning back and as an afterthought applauding them, it was little consolation. Being accompaniment for Lolly not only infuriated them, it made them even hotter in the afternoon sun than they might have been. And they could not, hard as they marched, catch up with her. Perspiring beneath the long sleeves of their white satin uniforms, the top fatty wedge of their thighs chafed and raw from constantly rubbing in the same place . . . same place . . .

same place . . . against one another, they marched like hot
little soldiers, trying not to see Lolly way ahead of them
floating back and forth free as a dream, her hair shining and
loose, jiving up and down and over and across potholed
half-cobblestoned old Main Street, turning, flipping, kicking,
leaping, twitching, sashaying her butt in their faces without
a stumble or fall in her body.

Two Eunola residents were not at the parade, had in fact
seen Lolly perform only one time on a Friday afternoon.
Her father, Frank Lasswell, was back at the high school in
his car, her school clothes draped over the seat next to him,
waiting for her to get finished so he could take her home for
dinner. Her mother was home in the trailer watching the
last daytime television serial of the day.

"Can you believe it?" Sid Strunk said as if for the first
time when Lolly passed his furniture and appliance store.
"That girl was raised in a trailer house!" He said it every
time she passed, every Friday of football season repeated
those exact words. Part of the legend being the estab-
lishment of the language which, once done, remained im-
peccably unchanged. Part of the dream the astonishment
that where she came from had not determined her destiny.
That she had not become—like every other girl from the
trailer park—a trailer tramp. That in his time as well Graham, a Cunningham, had rejected family advantage to go
into the business of keeping a drunk on. That Booth Oates's
family was a severely quiet and respectful one, who had yet
produced one son, an idiot. Who, because he was *their* idiot,
the town took care of. That their whore, Alberta, put on her
hat and shopped with the best of them, demanding proper
service, which was unhesitatingly given. All four outside

regular social considerations, outside family and church . . .
outside.

Two blocks before the levee, at the Delta Theater . . .
known for its rats, B-grade black and white movies, and a
pervert who sat against the left-hand wall waiting for col-
leagues and strangers . . . somebody yelled to Lolly to
throw up her baton. She and the little girl on the sidewalk
both did, and as Lolly leaned toward one knee, keeping a
perfect balance between the strain of her body on the street
and the silver stick moving against the force of its own iner-
tia, she found her focus. Not on the baton itself but its aura,
that stream of silver that when the baton was going fast
enough caught up with itself and made a solid round of silver in the air. That dazzling exhaust; it kept her attention.
Pure chance, from pure perfection. She thought concentrating on it would take her past where she was now, past all
the ribbons and trophies she had already won, past being
the substantiation of a dream for a town she disdained into
being . . . the Lolly Ray Lasswell . . . of the *world*, somehow. She caught the baton and moved on, and the man
who had called out for her to throw it beamed as if he had
done it himself.

Behind the band another group turned from Hawthorne
to Main. The Homecoming Court. It was Homecoming, and
the queen and her six maids also trailed Lolly.

At the end of Main in front of the levee, the city had
erected a statue in honor of its World War II dead. Some
city fathers designed it, which, to Eunola's chagrin, was exactly what it ended up looking like, a statue designed by a
committee. It was supposed to represent a warship. And you
could tell it was a ship all right, but it looked more like one
a child might draw than what any adult would design:

trapezoid with top line longer than bottom, straight line
sticking out the top, square attached to line, stars and
stripes inside the square. If a child drew that, you'd say
good, fine. But as a memorial, it was a monstrosity, an em-
barrassment. Which everyone saw every time he or she
drove down Main toward the levee. It was made of white
tile bordered in blue, and across the top of the memorial just
under the border it had said for years now "TO T OSE
WHO PROU LY ERV D IN ME RIAM." The missing letters had either fallen or been stolen and since the war by
now had been pretty much relegated to past history and
nobody wanted to fool with that memorial anyway, they
had not been replaced. Listed under that message were the
names of every white Eunolite who died in World War II.

When Lolly got close to the memorial, she tossed her hair
out of her eyes and looked, for the first time, into the crowd.
The statue stood directly in front of the levee, and as the
levee blocked off the sun a little when she got close enough
to it, she could look straight into the faces there. She was actually searching for a name on the memorial, Cecil Cyril
DeLoach, against which he usually leaned. When she found
it, he was not there. But he had never missed. Then she saw
his wings glint, on the other side, to the left. There. He had
moved; he was directly in front of Morris Leon Grizzanti,
leaning on the second z. Morris' brothers and sisters now ran
a pizza place near the trailer park. And the smile flooding
over Lolly's face then was as pure as a baby's. Unclouded
joy spread like a blush. He wore mirrored sunglasses and silver wings on his air force shirt, both of which picked up
what sunlight they could from that angle and flashed it at
her, just as she was flashing to the crowds up and down the
street. That was what had caught her eye the first time, and

while she hadn't been able to see his eyes for those strange
silver glasses—and still hadn't—he had signaled her with a
cocky two-finger salute, which, combined with the way he
grinned at her and the slouchy way he leaned against the
memorial, had established him in her mind as a collaborator.
He knew what she was up to, it seemed, her contrivance and
plans, and saw beyond what the others did. And saluted her
for it. After that first time she looked for him every Friday
there and acknowledged his presence with—besides that
spectacular smile—a special heel-toe jiving dance step and
an over-the-baton jump before turning left down River
Road toward Court where she would turn left again and
head, sun behind her, toward the high school she had
started from.

Above the wings, though Lolly couldn't see it, a blue plastic tab announced her compatriot's name, which was Lt.
James Blue. Lieutenant Blue came to see Lolly every Friday
and never waited to see a single majorette.

Once the sun gave up and started sinking into the levee,
the air cooled off a little and people felt a little easier standing on the concrete. Still, those lining Court had to look into
the half-sun's blurred glow to see Lolly, and the majorettes
still squinched their eyes up as they neared the end of Main.
Lolly's performance never let up, but because the people on
Court were a little less fanatic than those on Main, whose
compulsion was not only to see her but to see her *first*, she
gave them less. Some of the Mains came over to Court, however, and on the corners where they shouted to her she did a
special trick, like bending herself backward until her head
came down between her feet and all they could see was half
her body with its head between its legs and two silver sticks
turning beside it. Others went on home, some to prepare

dinner and return to the stadium behind the high school, where she would twirl again at halftime. As it was Homecoming, crowds would be heavier than usual.

Frank Lasswell waited patiently for his daughter. From the sun's near disappearance he knew she'd be coming soon. Smoking, easing ashes off the end of his cigarette with his middle finger, he gave the impression of a tough and leathery, unapproachable old man. Parked over the railroad tracks in front of the school, he would see her just before she climbed the hump the tracks ran on, one split second where Court Street curved, then would lose her behind the hump. When she got high enough he would see her again, coming up like fireworks.

He neither understood nor liked what Lolly did. She had little idea what she risked, stirring people up, and little notion what they were capable of, once aroused. He didn't watch her in the parades because he couldn't stand to. He was vulnerable where she was concerned, and inside his stony chest his heart leaped and fell with her tricks and stunts. But she had worked so hard. He had seen her day after day from the time she was ten years old, turning first a broomstick then a baton around and around until her fingers ached. And when he had asked if she wanted to go to twirling camps and classes and she had refused and said she didn't need them, he had understood. Doing it on her own made her proud. It enabled her to have what she had worked for for herself, setting her off from the town. And so he said nothing of his skepticism, and helped her every way he knew how.

When he saw her on the tracks, her chin high, he thought she looked like Lucille . . . though Lucille had never done anything remotely similar to twirling a baton. When she hit the top of the tracks she turned around on one toe then stopped stock still between the ties. Her eyes were on Frank, her chin was out and up and long, her shoulders were back, and from up there she was looking out as if over a countryside that belonged exclusively to *her*. At that moment, she had the look of a Peavey. His wife's people. That fierce and uncontainable pride that bordered on hatred. If, that is, a Peavey had ever in his life owned anything to overlook besides his own delusions. It unnerved Frank.

At home, Lucille stirred the stew and checked the cornbread, which she was warming from lunch. Although she was not watching it, the television set filled the trailer with sounds of cartoon characters. The table was set for three, and every now and then Lucille ran a hand through her long curly graying hair and moaned softly. Her head hurt again.

After Lolly did her turn atop the railroad tracks, she was through . . . the act was over . . . and when she ran like a child to her father and asked if she could please drive home, it was as if a mask had been taken off.

"No," he said briskly, "get in; we have to hurry." Not meaning to be short with her but still off-balance from seeing the Peavey in her.

But when she rounded the front of the car and coyly stuck her tongue out at him, looking across the car hood from the sides of her eyes, his face uncrinkled, he shot out a loving hand urging her to come take his place, and, bewitched, slid across.

She patted his leg softly when she got in, then pulled away from the curb. When they turned the corner just before the tracks, the majorettes were cresting the hump, perspiration running like rain from beneath their hats. Lolly glanced at them but did not wave or speak, and neither did they.

Behind the band and the Homecoming Court, the sun had finally dropped from sight. Only its fierce red and gold afterglow remained, its last gasp before sinking into the river and yielding to the north wind, which drew near. Clouds which had all day puffed and billowed themselves about like soap bubbles were now stretched out thin, and with the sun's light coming up through them their whiteness had turned into bright, hard colors, red, orange, and a violent pink. Like cheap teasing dimestore scarves they discreetly covered the sun's decline.

Lucille was sitting at the table waiting for them, angry. Dinner was on the table, the bowls on cardboard pads to protect the maple finish; the iced tea was poured, the ice melting; the cornbread still in the oven, which she had neglected to turn on.

She liked to be in the trailer alone. Days she didn't have headaches she was quite happy there, wandering room to room all day, sniffing out corners, going through Lolly's belongings, watching television games and serials. She re-sewed sequins on Lolly's gold costume and polished her silver boots; mended her clothes, washed and ironed them expertly; tasted her daughter's life the only way she knew how or was allowed to, like a burglar. But Lolly took good care of herself and had so little need for her mother that Lucille sometimes invaded the neatness of her daughter's room, put it in disarray, and came back later on in the day to survey the disorder and set about straightening it.

They were late, she thought, again. They were always late.

She got up and took the cold cornbread out of the oven, and, back at the table, stared at the door they would come through.

She expected they were afraid to ask what she did all day alone, either that or they didn't care; at any rate they never asked, which was just as well. If they knew how content she was, how well she operated there . . . if they saw her even smile occasionally at the antics of some TV clown when they had not seen her smile in years . . . they might think her capable of getting on better with them and with others, they would expect more of her, and she could not take on anything other than what she was handling now. There was a sign outside the trailer, pushed into the ground next to the steps, that said, "Lucille Lasswell, Sewing," but nobody ever came with work for her to do any more. She used to sew, not scratch sewing, nothing new, only alterations, lifting and lowering hems, taking in, letting out, patching, turning collars, until one day the seams in front of her merged like cracks in the earth turning this way and that going nowhere, and she had run the machine up and down somebody's dress and ruined it. From then on nobody came. Well, she thought, it was just as well. It was all she could do to get through the afternoon serials—they sometimes depressed her so—which ran from noon to four. By the time Frank and Lolly got home at four-thirty, she would have retired to bed to prepare herself for the night with them. Lying there staring at her hands, pushing back the cuticles, admiring her long slender fingers, the skin taut and shiny across the knuckles . . . beautiful hands, a piano teacher had once told her, talented fingers . . . running a palm gently against those knuckles, she felt fine and peaceful actually until she heard the trailer door unlocked and opened.

Her footsteps came first, rapid and clicking in those clickety
shoes she bought with pennies slid into slots above the arch.
Strange shoes, Lucille thought, to have slots in them for
pennies. Then his, heavy, solid, from his work boots, with
the silver plates across the toes . . . dirty, no doubt. And the
door, the terrible sound she had never gotten used to, after
all the years living in a trailer. Like the door to a meat
locker, it echoed metallic sounds, clasps, locks, buttons, aluminum frames . . . a terrible *clunch* sound . . . the closing
of an airtight container, all that was inside now sealed up. It
took her breath away to think of it. And since windows were
never opened because of their fancy central air conditioning
and heat, everything inside stayed inside.

A trailer house was simply not substantial enough for her,
who when she walked the earth felt it tremble beneath her,
who feared in a light wind the threat of a tornado. For one
who trusted neither nature nor life itself, a trailer was simply not secure enough that she could ever feel comfortable
in it.

She became a mad sullen woman then, outraged, crazy, as
heavy as a stone. With the closing of the door, the rage
which ruled her life moved up and encased her and her
night began. It was as though a dark hood had descended.
It would not come off again until they were gone again the
next morning and she was alone, free to work inside her own
rhythms and reality. The rage fed her and kept her in a day-
to-day cycle she could manage. Anger kept her going; bitterness was her solace. Without either, she'd have taken to
her bed and not got up.

Fridays, however, were different. Frank had asked if during football season she could possibly manage to have dinner ready when they got home on Fridays after the parade

and she had said she would. And so every Friday she was
sitting at the table waiting for them when they arrived, dinner cold, having been ready half an hour before they got
there, even though she knew what time they would come.
She sat leaning on one elbow, the table meticulously set,
napkins folded in half beneath the forks, spoons to the right
of knives, glasses perspiring into coasters, glaring at them
when they walked in, as if to say, I have done what you
have demanded of me and now you are late . . . late. *Why
are you doing these things to me?*

The depths and complexities of her personality mystified
Frank entirely. He knew only to pacify her then let her
be. Lolly ignored her as much as possible, almost entirely.

Frank greeted Lucille as if she might respond—he always
gave her that chance though she never did—then sat to eat.
Lolly went quickly into her bedroom to take off her costume
and boots and put on a loose robe, and the three began their
dinner together. It was stew again, and cornbread butter
wouldn't melt on, which held in their mouths like pure
starch. Frank had asked her not to make more stews, they
were tired of stew, but no matter what kind of meat he
brought home, she insisted on turning it into stew. Tasteless,
stringy, full of soft grainy potatoes and mealy carrot slices
and whole canned tomatoes floating like small drowned
bodies: even her meals spoke her anger. Lucille said nothing, but slurped up juices and kept her head down while
Frank and Lolly talked, he about her school, she the parade.

Outside, children ran behind the trailers and between, resisting oncoming darkness as well as their mothers' shouts to
come in, it was getting dark. Fifteen miles above them,
where the river crooked and turned like a child's scribbles,

the north wind came down, blew across the water, and shivered inside the trees.

It was a big trailer, with wall-to-wall carpeting, central air and heat, major appliances, and two bedrooms. Good enough, Frank had said, for anybody. Good enough and plenty enough of anything anybody needed to get by comfortably enough.

Frank's family had lived in a town like Eunola, a hundred miles south on the river. His grandfather had come there looking for an easier life than he could make for himself and his family on the Texas plains, where the ground froze and the dry wind drew what little moisture there was out of the ground and left them year after year with little to show for their hard work. So he sold what he had and brought his family to a settlement of homes outside a town about the size of Eunola. There was less land to work there, but it was fertile. Frank's grandfather had told him he had wanted to be near the river "where the land is rich and a man don't have to kill himself trying to wet it because the wetness is already there, especially where the land is flat and has received the river's bounty. There, the land is waiting for the seed, is ready for it and ripe for it. *Meant* for it."

Where a man could, he said, if he stood long enough, plant his own feet in the ground and grow something out the top of his head.

Frank thought his grandfather did well enough back then, looking only to get through and maybe if he was lucky end up with a little more to show for his pains and a little less pain getting it than he had been used to . . . nothing more. But small farms were being eased out and Frank's grandfather had died in town in the bottom tier of Frank's bunk beds and so in the end his convictions hadn't come to much. Except that he had had them. Which was something.

Aaron, Frank's father, craved something more. After marrying, he had moved immediately into town, leaving behind the reason for coming into that particular part of the country in the first place, discounting the need for the land's fertility his father had come there to enjoy, and so the town could have been any town anyplace. It was town, was all. And if the trees were more luxuriant and the summer longer in that part of the country than in some others, it didn't really make that much difference. It was town and Frank hated it. The only happy childhood times he remembered were the visits out to the farm his grandfather kept until his grandmother died and the old man finally moved in with them. Aaron Lasswell was a hard worker and an ambitious man. He went to work pumping gas at a filling station and it wasn't long before he was managing it and another just like it across town. If his father hadn't had that streak in him that wanted more, that something which pushed him past being satisfied to make his way and hold to what he had, it would have been at least bearable and Frank would have stayed. But Aaron craved being a part of town and that was all town meant to Frank, that unfulfilled urge. Aaron yearned to be *accepted*. Which he could not and was never going to be, no matter how much gas he pumped or windows he polished or how many opinions on weather, the football team, or the state of the world he agreed with. And Frank's mother, who got worn out fast, just went along. Whatever Aaron said was right to do, she did.

Frank had watched his parents struggle to maintain the standards of respectability and acceptability the town prescribed. They painted it on like a thick coat of varnish slapped on a beat-up table, the oldness and cheapness of

which—the ugliness—would always show through. They
were what townspeople called rednecks, which was never
going to change because like the red "V" on his father's
chest from being out in the sun in an open-neck shirt so
many years . . . his chest pale as watered milk, the bottoms
of his feet as soft and pink as a baby's . . . it had become
permanent.

He watched his father on Sundays put on the same suit
and tie year after year, long past its time of good use and
fashion, and go off to the Methodist church where he—a
Baptist baptized by submersion—knelt for communions and
sang stiff Wesleyan hymns and watched babies christened
with a few pitiful drops of water, not saved for life by that
moistening but only protected for a while, set on the road
until they were old enough to decide for themselves
whether or not to stay on it, instead of being SAVED in
some mystical way forever, because Methodist was a more
acceptable religion in town. He watched his mother volun-
teer too late for Girl Scout leadership when all the better
girls had dropped out of Scouts and gone to more socialized
activities like Cotillion Clubs and the only ones left to scout
were overweight, unsociable, or too intense . . . or were
country girls like his sister who could plant and cook and
raise chickens with ease, none of which was valued by the
people she wanted to run with. Frank himself had felt the
shame of riding in a car not quite equal to the other kids'
and yet—and here was the crux of it, the thing that Frank
was determined to avoid—they had a car, a house, did go to
church, did vote. Were trying to be what others were, and
while poor from that trying, were never getting an inch
closer.

Frank left home at fifteen before finishing high school, the day after his grandfather died, and had never gone back. He didn't know what had become of any of them. And rarely cared. He couldn't afford it. He'd come to Eunola, saved up and bought himself a small trailer, and determined what he would not do: he would not repeat his father's mistakes. He would not be deluded by dreams or be made a fool of by excessive hope. He would make his way and be done. He would above all hold on, and keep his life ordered, would have as little to do with people in town as possible, would be nothing other than what he was. He would neither wag nor jump nor sit up for fortune, holding out hope like a biscuit just enough out of his reach that he'd have to leap for it. Frank, only fifteen, lay awake nights thinking these things out; first in the boardinghouse when he was pumping gas and later, in his own one-room trailer when he got the job in the gravel pits he still had twenty-five years later.

And Frank and Lucille could not now be called poor by anybody. They had insurance, a savings account, full suites of bedroom, living room, and dining room furniture, and he was able to trade in his moderately priced car every three to four years. All because, he said, he knew when enough was enough. When it came down to it, a man had to make for himself the best terms with life he could and then work within the framework those terms established, like an insurance contract or bank loan, with rewards and punishments clearly stated. You had to accept shortcomings and disadvantages and deal with them as you could, not as you might if you only had more. And you never borrowed against possibilities, only against hard facts, present and visible. There was no mystery: you did it. Frank believed that.

"Nobody can ever accuse Frank Lasswell of trying to be something he's not," he often told Lolly, speaking of himself

as if he could see Frank Lasswell's life apart from himself,
something he had built and could refer to, as if it were a
house or a fence. Not flaunting it or degrading it, but rea-
sonably proud.

Lucille looked up only once from her stew . . . when
Lolly mentioned that since it was Homecoming there would
be a big crowd and they should start out early.

"You the queen?" Lucille asked sarcastically.

Lolly said nothing but kept eating as if no one had spoken
and Lucille went back to her meal.

Her long chin, with a point like a valentine's tip, was even
with the bowl and she was slurping and sucking the stew
into her mouth as if to make as much noise as possible. When there was only a spoonful left she broke off a
piece of cornbread down into it and watched as the red
juice soaked in, then crumbled the piece with her spoon and
ate that as lovingly as she had the stringy meat and potatoes.

As she swallowed the last spoonful, she sighed deep in her
throat like a dog settling in sleep.

No eye contact was made between Lucille and the other
two during the meal. Lucille would not stand for it; she
made a terrible scene if she ever caught one of them—or
anybody else, for that matter—at it. Used to be, they'd go
out sometimes to a barbecue place or Grizzanti's for pizza,
but it got so every time they went Lucille insisted somebody
was staring at her and then would make a scene, staring
back at the person with ferocity, whispering to Lolly and
Frank how expertly she was getting her revenge (the enemy
was always a woman, usually a waitress), until they felt

forced to leave. So now they ate at home and Lucille went nowhere. Not to the store, not out for a drive, nowhere. She did not answer the telephone when it rang and had only once, at Frank's insistence, seen Lolly twirl. That one time it made her sick, literally, to her stomach, and gave her a violent headache.

When Lolly went outside to practice her routine for the night, Frank and Lucille began to clear the table. Neither spoke, but when Frank began to whistle out the side of his mouth—casually, a man who for company whistles to himself—Lucille immediately put her hand to her head, as if the sound was piercing her skull, still not looking at him or directly accusing him of anything.

"Lucille, why don't you go on and lie down. I'll finish this."

With that, she rubbed the table harder. He could see her head was boiling. Her resentment and bitterness were so old to Frank he had grown used to them, like a birthmark, like work or weather, or the on and on, day to day getting on with what there was to do, like anything inevitable and unchanging.

Frank kept whistling, softer now, smokier.

When they married, Frank had thought Lucille's edgy high-strung nervousness was caused by her mother, Mrs. Peavey, who had beat her until the day they married and even then was ready to tear off a limb and thrash her when she found out they'd done it . . . even though Lucille wasn't living at home any more. But Frank had held the old woman's arm down and said, "That's enough, Mrs. Peavey. I'm in charge of Lucille now." She'd have enjoyed hitting Frank then, but since he wasn't Peavey and none of her concern, she had withdrawn in a huff. Still, Lucille had stayed

with her arms over her head, leaning against the side of the
house, to protect herself from her mother's rage.

She had been so beautiful. Only sixteen, she had looked
wary and unfinished, like a colt stumbling about wild-eyed,
trying to walk straight. The youngest of eight surviving Peavey children, the least wanted child, she had been sent from
home to her older sister Ola Faye's house to help take care
of her babies and house, while another older brother and
sister were still at home. Frank had come by to pick up
Lucille's brother-in-law for work, not knowing she was
there. She had been ironing in the kitchen. When he by
habit opened the kitchen door without knocking, she had
been startled . . . he could still see her, backed up against
the wall, one hand over her mouth, the other clutching the
iron, her eyes so serious and afraid. Then she was embarrassed at having been revealed in front of him, a stranger,
letting him know so straightforwardly how she felt. She had
blushed deeply. Her short dark hair had curled provoca-
tively about her face, framing it, and there was something in
her eyes that thrilled Frank. The energy there, behind those
large deep-set eyes hooded over with such heavily rounded
lids, the spirit, the vibrancy. He had been lonely in his
trailer. Marrying Lucille had been his one concession to a
dream: an option for the unknown, for the possible, unknown factors outside the contract he had drawn up.

She had wanted to finish high school, which after they
were married she was able to do. He remembered how dili-
gently she worked over her schoolbooks and how she looked
when she brought home good grades. He would come in
from work and find her report card propped against the
sugar bowl for him to see, folded open so the A's and B's
would show. She had been so bright and expectant, so tall

and gawky . . . and young, younger than he'd ever known
how to be.

Frank thought now he might have done everything all
wrong but he had done all he had known how to at the time.
He had tried to be gentle with her, at the same time insist-
ing she establish some *order* in her life so that she could
grow up out of her wildness, come out of that Peavey craziness into a sane, reasoning person who had some measure
of control over her life. He had only meant to help her. She
had ducked her head when he said those things, like a child
promising to be good and never do it again, whatever *it*
might be, which he realized she never knew, intimating:
now that you've told me what bad is, I'll be good.

Then something happened. Between her school days and
Lolly's birth, some gap widened and Lucille plunged, and
her head began to boil. By the third year of their marriage,
when she became pregnant, Frank could see that he had
been mistaken thinking she would get better. She screamed
in pain during each menstrual period—pain he told her she
was only making worse by thrashing about on the bed the
way she did, to which she had replied, sitting board straight
on the bed, her hand on her belly, her eyes aflame, *How
would you know?* not as a question but a summation, flatly
irrefutable. (Lucille was baffled by the things that made
her, things of her sex, the blood, the shaved hair, the eggs
cycling, the utter helplessness in the face of it all; these were
hateful to her; she could not accommodate them into her
life or find a way to absorb their burden.)

After that, he learned to anticipate her periods and, when
they came, to be out of the trailer as much as possible. But
those times were nothing compared to the silence with
which she punished him during her pregnancy. She never

bought a single piece of baby clothing and never made one. No bed, nothing. Frank did it all. She only sat and stared at him, in deep resentment, the like of which he had only seen in one other person, her mother, Mrs. Peavey.

Life was no contract to Peaveys but a wild thing to be wrestled, scratched, clawed, kicked, spat on, struggled with, however one might manage, with few rules to contain the violence, because as your opponent had such clear advantage there was no way to win. The point was not winning anyway; the point was fighting tooth and nail as long as you had breath left in you to fight and not *for* anything either, only keeping it going because the fight was all there was. Peaveys died panting, struggling to get up for more, their eyes bulging with strain, every muscle protesting it being over. They never expected to win and in the end did not feel defeated—because there was no defeat just as there had never been a possibility of victory—only disappointed. It was the ending of it they hated. Just that. And since they never let down their defenses for fear of being struck from behind, there was not much joy in their lives or rest. How long you stayed was the only measure of success they recognized, that and the fierceness of your fight. Peavey women ranted and raged even more ferociously than the men, having a greater store of fury than physical strength, feeling eternally cheated that that was so. The women were the craziest, Frank thought; they died either screaming or dead silent, sinister.

After the baby was born, Lucille had retired into the bedroom. She sewed there, listening to the radio, then later on watched television, nursing the headaches which started soon after. She became totally inaccessible to Frank then and to Lolly as well. She closed herself off and had stayed

that way. The dark hood was down. Frank, hoping to stave
off some of the Peavey craziness, took the baby and raised it
himself. He worked night shifts while Lolly was little, sleeping when the child did: short naps in the afternoon and from
seven, when he tucked her in, until eleven-thirty at night,
when he slipped out of the trailer carrying his silver hard
hat, which Lolly loved. He kept it inside during the day for
her to play with.

She had been a sweet, docile child. She had stayed close
to the trailer, and to him, and had never ventured farther
than he allowed her to go. She liked to play inside, and
made up games and lives for herself and her dolls there, as
the trailer alternately became a castle, the grocery store, an
operating room. She kept herself neat and clean, even as a
child, and never liked even her feet to be dirty.

When they were through cleaning, Lucille poured four
Empirin tablets into her palm and filled a tall glass full of
tap water. She sometimes took as many as twenty pills a
day. She would not go to the doctor or take substitutes; Empirin, she said, took care of her. As he made coffee, Frank
watched her put the tablets one by one on her tongue and
swallowing great gulps of water with each, take them lovingly, as if feeding a child. Absorbed, she did not notice him
watching her, or if she did, gave no sign of it. Then without
a word she went back to their bedroom, holding the palm
of her hand flat against the topmost curve of her forehead. The sight of her in pain still grieved Frank, much as
he tried to let it pass over him. Sitting by the front picture
window, waiting for the coffee to make, he watched Lolly
practice.

She twirled halfheartedly, thinking of the air force lieutenant leaning back against the memorial, so sure of himself, saluting her like that, as if looking deep inside her. She wondered how he knew so much, if he did. When Frank came out to tell her she had only fifteen more minutes before they had to leave, he looked up into the trees. The leaves were barely trembling, but he could feel anticipation ruffling them.

"It'll be here soon."

Lolly looked up but could see nothing. "What?"

Frank couldn't understand people living in the weather without taking notice of it. Eunolites never seemed to note any wind change outside a tornado or a snowstorm, and even then they practically had to be carried off bodily to pay much attention. Frank could taste the change before it came, could smell it, thin in the air like distant smoke. If his father had stayed on the farm, he could have used that ability, because they'd have had to watch for weather changes. His grandfather used to point his cane when the cows lay with their legs buckled under them, their heads low, quietly herded together in bunches. It meant, he said, cold weather was coming. They were storing energy, saving the warmth in their fat for the time ahead, when they would need it. It was a sign to those who recognized it, who needed to know what it meant.

"Now, Lolly," Frank chided her. "I know I taught you . . ."

"The wind." She interrupted him. "Good. I twirl better when it's cool." Which was probably more than it meant to anybody else in town, or at least as much.

"Don't wait too long," he said, and turning back, went in to get his coffee.

Lolly tried to remember what she had been thinking of when Frank came out and interrupted her, but since she couldn't, she assumed it wasn't important and, listlessly turning the silver stick under her arm, went to get dressed.

The night, by the time they got to the stadium, was perfect for a Homecoming. The air was clear and cool, the sky was black; a fat gold moon lay low on the horizon, and big withered sycamore leaves flew in the new north wind like empty hands palm up. The returning former EHS students walked to the stadium through the leaves, crunching them apart into splinters and shards on the concrete, not noticing as they played student again, romping, joking, drinking, and yelling old cheers, waving their felt pennants . . . against the relentless fact of approaching winter, against the dying of the leaves, as if they could by going back revive their first buddings and stave off the winter whose faint stirring could be sensed inside the occasionally harder gust of wind that blew free across the bright empty playing field. Inside the autumn breeze a funnel of bitter cold turned, menacing their cheer. It ruffled the streamers hanging from goal posts and chilled majorettes' bare chafed legs. Frank, standing by the fence in his usual place behind the goal post, zipped his brown leather jacket halfway up against the chill, his eyes on Lolly, about whom warmth hung like an aura.

She stood at the gate to the field, all intensity and concentration.

Like cows, he thought, she stores it for when she needs it.

It was halftime, and as the players hustled off and the band gathered behind her, she waited at the gate for the

exact moment when something inside told her it was time to
move out. Because her sense of this was more accurate than
his, the band director had deferred to her, in a rare show of
humility, and it was she who decided when the halftime
performance began. She looked warm in the night chill.
Only the Homecoming Queen, whose shoulders were bare,
seemed as immune to the cold.

Frank felt a mild roar of illness in his lower gut. The
stands were filled to overflowing with a Homecoming crowd
that, having seen a losing first half, trembled for a halftime
show that would redeem the evening. Such foolishness. The
queen and her court wore long rainbow pastel evening
gowns, which had been spread across the back of four convertibles. The girls sat atop the back seats of the cars. The
queen was alone in hers, and there were two maids in each
of the others, driven by selected town dignitaries . . . old
men, their faces pink with excitement, their lank jowls quivering . . . who also awaited Lolly's signal. Foolishness,
Frank thought, watching the girls correct their lipstick and
hair. For adults to indulge in nonsense children might be allowed was pure foolishness. They filled the stands, with
their flasks of bourbon and new fall corduroys and dreams
of grandeur their children were expected to fulfill. It was
too late for them . . . and so they laid their hopes elsewhere, and the quality of the football coach's very life hung
on his ability to serve them up that dream to suit them. If he
did it well, he received generous favors, anonymous dona-
tions, a car, a cashmere coat, money . . . concrete proofs of
gratitude. But if he did not, he risked the fate of the last
Hornet coach, who after five straight losses, one a humili-
ating 38–0 defeat on the home field, was burned in effigy on
his own front lawn, as his wife and children watched, and

fired, midseason, and asked to leave town. The game was serious.

The moment arrived.

Frank could tell by the transformation Lolly went through: she became a Lolly he did not know, who bore no resemblance to the quiet sweet child making up names and people and places, obeying him sweetly. First she threw her head back. Then she put on her smiling mask and pushed her breasts high and arched her back in a perfect, startling C, so that her hair hung down near the ground and her head was curved toward her butt. One leg shot straight out from her body, and the arm carrying her baton went up over her, the other one reaching hard down toward the ground behind. She held nothing back now. Everything was part of the moment, to which she was totally committed . . . this time, *now*. It was uncanny the way she did it, her rapport with time itself, as if she became a part of it and knew without thinking what was to come next and how long to hold each pose, turn each way, stand without moving. At that, the drummers, having received their signal, began playing, and she was off. The ill feeling spread in Frank . . . rose up . . . and he turned and went through the crowd to the concession stand to get a cup of coffee.

In line, someone touched his shoulder.

"Excuse me."

Frank moved aside.

"No . . . Mr. Lasswell . . . ?"

A young man in uniform spoke to him. Frank had not expected it. He rarely talked with anyone at the games, and few ever approached him.

"Excuse me . . . are you . . . ?"

"Yes, I'm Frank Lasswell. Can I help you?"

"I'm James Blue."

The young man held out his hand for Frank to shake, his eyes steady and blue and piercingly sure.

"I hope I'm not intruding," he went on, "but I saw you coming in with Lolly and assumed you must be her father. I wanted to speak with you, if you don't mind."

Frank knew how the town felt about the air force base and their girls, how the two were not to mix, but he returned the lieutenant's politeness. Lolly never dated high school boys anyway, and so he didn't see how it could hurt, especially since she was a senior. Frank bought Blue a coffee. Right off, he liked him.

By the time they got back to the fence together, coffee in hand, Lolly was midfield of the fifty-yard line, executing a particularly intricate set of spectacular twirling maneuvers. Frank sipped his coffee and watched, as people yelled her name and screamed. The convertibles carrying the seven gowned girls moved slowly around and around the field, as the girls waved into the stands, circling Lolly as if in tribute, while the band—divided in half, some at one end, some at the other—played a march tune. The majorettes twirled clumsily, flanking the two sections of the band, and smiled so hard their mouths twitched. The queen, her red lips shining, cradled her bouquet of shaggy chrysanthemums as if it were a bundled baby and waved her gloved hand stiffly in her best imitation of regality. First the fullback's, then the right halfback's, then the quarterback's steady girl, she had been working toward this moment for three years and, her maids whispered among themselves, she had done everything in the book to earn the title. It was, for her, a heady moment.

And Lolly knew it.

She threw her baton in a lateral twirl so high up it took
the audience's attention from the convertibles and didn't
give it back. Over the lights, over the trees, the silver stick
turned against the black night sky like a new star, like a silver toothpick, like a rising hope, a new moon, and the people's heads went back as it rose. Their eyes left the queen
and went from the baton down to Lolly, from Lolly back up
to the baton. Standing feet straddled, arms outstretched,
glittering in the field lights, as gold as the fat autumn moon
low on the horizon, confident now, unwilling, unable, not
destined to fail—it not being in her at this point in her life to
fail—she dared do a trick she had never practiced. The time
called for it. As the baton turned above her, she flipped her
body upside down, shifted her contact with the earth from
feet to hands, her legs together pointing straight up in the
direction of the baton, then—when she felt the baton had
peaked and was starting to fall—turned over, bent her back,
and went down onto the field in a split, each toe pointing at
a different stand. At that moment she looked up to see the
baton exactly where it should have been, slightly above her
head, and just in time caught it there, split apart on the
field. The crowd went wild, shouting her name, applauding,
passing silver flasks one to the other, beating fists against the
air the way they did when a football player streaked out of a
crush toward the goal line. And Lolly held herself there, her
legs out and her arms up over her head in triumph, turning
from stand to stand, flashing them the smile of promise they
came for. It was what they screamed and bayed and lusted
for: the promise. Of that which they might have been but
weren't and felt no longer capable of, of what could be but
rarely was, of wonder, astonishment, illumination: a promise
of dreams larger and bolder than they themselves dared

dream. Of *love* . . . that too . . . and of being loved. Lolly gave them all that with her twirling and her smile . . . with the very presence of her down on the field so unrepentantly brazen in her pursuit of glory . . . even though she didn't know, but only felt the rightness, and did it. A promise of necessity not to be fulfilled and therefore not to be spoiled.

Frank averted his eyes, while James Blue's stayed coolly on her. Just at that moment, the queen . . . not sensing . . . started from her car, headed for her coronation, which was to take place exactly where Lolly was, square in the middle of the field.

As she made her first step from the car, the door frame caught her heel and she tripped and fell forward into the arms of her escort and in an effort to keep herself from falling to the ground, crushed his fingers together. He winced, eyes bugged. Trapped chrysanthemums shed petals about his feet. Frantically she pushed against him to right herself, and once composed, looked quickly up into the stands to see if her awkwardness had been noticed. But no one was looking. Even the mayor, who moved onto the field now, had directed his attention toward the gold and silver twirler spread apart on the fifty-yard line, Eunola's own Lolly Ray Lasswell. Only Sid Strunk's eight-year-old son Thorne, who was behind the mayor carrying the queen's rhinestone tiara on a black and gold velvet pillow, saw the near accident and giggled red-faced about it throughout the coronation.

And as Frank was saying yes, if it was all right with Lolly, Lieutenant Blue could certainly pay a call, Lolly was handing the band director her baton so that she could flip-flop in one handstand after the other off the field, as the crowd cheered and the queen waited, and Lucille was taking her eighteenth Empirin of the day and then her nineteenth, knowing they would soon be home, closing her eyes attempting to shut out the remains of that Friday before they got there. She held something in her hand. It was old now and worn, but clear. A picture. A family of children, stern-faced and wary, standing in a row flat across its breadth. They stared suspiciously out, holding on to what they had. Lucille could imagine someone herding them together to have it taken and·them saying what, what for, what is it, I don't want to. And then all of them together in a row, lined up, that same feeling spoken into the camera, that distrustfulness snapped, then taken off to be developed and turned into a picture, guardedness, fear, recorded now forever. In the middle of the rest, a baby sat in soft, light-colored dirt with tracks in it, a road. Naked except for diapers, the baby looked glowing and happy, the only one of the group not faced off to the death with the camera. Fearful, it seemed, of nothing, its head thrown back, its arms out, a halo of soft blond hair encircling its head, the baby seemed to be submitting joyously . . . to the camera, to the sky, sun, life, whatever there was now or to come. A boy of three or four, Felton, she thought, stood barefoot behind the baby as if in protection, and all around the brothers and sisters stood erect and stern, like soldiers. The rest of them looked so stiff, so hindered with life, so burdened by it, even as young as some of them were. Only the baby, that lump of dazzlement square in the center of the picture, looked *up* instead of out. There she was, the baby in the road in front of them, their one spark of hope that this was not all, this getting through. Lucille. Sitting in the dirt, happy.

She inspected the picture often, staring long and hard into it, trying to find in those sparkling eyes some key. Where was she now in that fat, laughing baby? Where was

Lucille? There must be a hint. And where was the dark
hood of her future?

On one end of the group, Mrs. Peavey stood like a sen-
tinel, square as a post. Defiance burning in her eyes, she
stared murderously out of the picture, her eyes pinpoints of
rage, her fury directed unflinchingly at that moment at the
camera . . . now, at whoever chanced to look her way. Lucille's father, Matthew, was not in it. She had no picture of
him. Lucille wondered who it was had wanted this one
made.

She fell asleep clutching it and awoke some hours later,
surprised to hear laughter in the trailer.

When Frank came to bed, she was not asleep, which he
knew. She was not ashamed of what she had done in front
of Frank, Lolly, and the stranger, at the same time that she
did not want a confrontation about it, and so feigned sleep.

Frank had undressed down to his undershorts and sat on
the side of the bed smoking a cigarette. James Blue had
impressed him favorably, he liked him, yet he was afraid.
He had seen Lolly look brazenly at Blue and knew he had
no right to be surprised or make accusations because he had
taught her not to be coy or evasive; she did not flirt with
boys the way other girls did. He had always thought it
would take a man to impress Lolly and now one had come
into their lives and he had been the one to invite him.

Lucille coughed. The smoke. He was always doing something, whistling, smoking, talking, even he thought living,
that she felt she must show him she hated.

The sight of Lucille coming from the bedroom, trailing
nightgown ruffles, her robe clutched loosely about her so
that one breast was plainly visible beneath the sheer nylon,

her hair as wild as flames, had embarrassed Lolly certainly, but Frank had welcomed the intrusion. On their way to the trailer they had stopped at a soft-custard ice cream stand and bought sundaes. When Lucille came in, Lolly was sucking and licking hers off her spoon in a way that was highly disturbing to Frank. With the red plastic spoon turned over so that the bowl of it fit against the roof of her mouth, she was slowly sucking ice cream off it. He saw Blue watching her. Then Lucille came in, and she looked beautiful to him, as wild and spirited as she had the first time he saw her.

Staring at a spot of light on the wall next to the bed, Lucille wondered how she had looked to them, a crazy woman, half-naked, streaking from her room, madness exuding from her like a bad smell, her dark hood all askew, a goofy hat falling off. Like Mama, she thought, and something broke apart in her chest as she thought it. I must have looked like Mama.

Frank rubbed out his cigarette and got in next to her. Her back was curled away from him as she lay on her side facing the wall, spine tucked down. Her knees were together, drawn up close to her belly, her hands under her face as if in prayer. Though she tried to be a crazy old woman, she was not old and when she relaxed and allowed you to look, you could see she was only thirty-seven, and still beautiful.

She pulled her knees up farther, waiting.

If he could help it, he wouldn't do it at all. But sometimes . . . he couldn't. He had been to whores, had paid for it daytimes while Lolly was in school and those times Lucille was so far away; during lunch hours and nighttimes instead of sleeping he had gone for it. But none had ever been as satisfying or as good as with Lucille. If she hadn't taken herself from him, he'd have never looked elsewhere. She was so

wild, so eager, so incredibly hungry . . . and hadn't known
what for, didn't know what was happening when the feeling
came and she fell across him moaning. She had excited him
coming into the living room as ferocious as only Peaveys
could be; he could still see the wildness. When he intro-
duced her to Blue, she said . . . nothing, not a word. But
only stared at him, eyes raging, arms crossed over her
breasts, that wild blue piercing Peavey look that made a
person think she knew everything he was or had ever
thought of; turned the look on Lolly, then back on Blue,
then left, streaking out like the wind. Lolly had been furious. Blue looked mystified . . . though not to Lucille; Lucille knew he had seen her from the first moment for what
she was, his avowed enemy, and recognized her entrance as
a statement of her hostility and a warning of its intensity.
Frank had been aroused.

Still, the urge seemed outside his contract; he ought to
have had more control.

He lifted her nightgown and without taking off his shorts
pushed himself up inside her. She was, as he had expected,
ready, had in fact been waiting for him. In a movement almost spasmodic, Lucille drew her knees even farther up and
bent her head down, clutching knees to chest. She didn't
move again, except to push down, to serve as an opposing
force to his thrust. Sounds rushed up out of her, and while
the rest of her body was still, the inside of her where Frank
was rippled and trembled, like falling water. Soon Frank
pushed harder and breathed audibly . . . which was all he
ever gave her, that one slightly hoarser breath, as if to say
this but no more, parceling out pleasure to her (or was it
parts of himself?) in small bits, like a parent worried about

tooth decay doling candy to a child. She stared at the wall and unwillingly gave up her secret raging.

They lay still a moment and then he pulled away and rearranged himself inside his shorts, turned from her and soon was asleep.

Lucille wept angrily as the warmth flowed out. It was the one thing they did together and neither of them could or ever had in twenty-one years admitted the need or dared look into the other one's eyes while it happened. She stared at the wall while his face was buried in her hair or she looked up over his shoulder—going back and forth—at the ceiling while he studied the sheet. They stole from one another . . . which was not so terrible, that was not it . . . what was so awful was their inability to admit the thievery and deceptions in order to get free of them. So the lies stuck. Like leeches, draining their blood. By now their bodies were spotted in an ordered and symmetrical polka dot and their blood was half gone.

Frank slept soundly but Lucille got up to take another pill and clean herself and wander through the trailer the rest of the night. Once, she went to Lolly's door, opened it, peeked in. She could see the gold uniform, hanging neatly on her closet door, the silver boots placed in line beneath it. The girl's eyes were closed and her breathing regular, but there was something studied about it and Lucille, whose senses were impeccable, felt sure she was awake.

By that time the Homecoming game was over, won by a last-minute EHS score, and the stadium, though still lit up, was empty. The Queen and her maids had gone on to the Hotel Eunola ballroom, where the dance would be held, while groups of jubilant parents and alumni went to various private parties and celebrations. The north wind blew in their faces as they walked quickly against it, those people who if anyone had asked how Eunola felt on a particular subject would have been the ones being referred to, as they were considered in important matters of opinion *the town*. They went to their parties and drank and laughed until they were drunk enough finally to go home.

There was unease in Eunola. A vague disquiet manifested in football games and parties, in stores and at the Yacht Club, at meeting grounds where common assumptions made behavior almost ritualistic in its sameness and capacity for repetition. People came to these places in a kind of frenzy now, as a wind of hysteria moved through them. It had not touched them deeply yet, but they felt whispers of it between them, like the foretaste of winter inside the north wind. And so they began forming groups, in the interest of their own interests. There were things they had always talked about that they still talked about, but with the slightest hesitation now, looking back over a shoulder to make sure no outsider was listening when the word passed. They were beginning . . . just beginning . . . to be afraid. Eunola was to know harder and more fearful times, they were only just at the brink of it now, but those who had smelled change had already set themselves stolidly against it, as stubborn as dinosaurs, sneering at those who let themselves be eased into new skin. Their dream was of containment, of stillness, sameness, of *stasis*. They meant to hold to what they had and yield nothing, to let nothing flow. But as tides change, winds shift, blood runs, the earth moves, the dream had to die. Their dream was also necessarily of stagnation, which the wind and time would not allow. Change was moving down on them as surely as the wind had. They had heard echoes of its consequences from north of them. From other parts of the country. From newspaper reports of decisions being made in cities far away. From outsiders . . . newspaper and television reporters who came and asked blankly what they intended doing when it happened to them. Some of them warned, these things will affect us, we must prepare ourselves. But most never believed it would reach them. They had no idea how their hearts were to be wrenched in the coming years.

Lolly would fail them, too. And when she did, when the promise she held out failed as well, they would shift their obsession from the change they could not face to her. Let loose their fears on her instead of the other, more terrible problem. In both, they would come to feel robbed of a dream they could never have explained and because of its being shared so unquestioningly had never had to. A dream the fulfillment of which *had* to be disappointing. The astonishment Lolly promised had finally to become jaded; Graham's beautiful drunkenness had to degenerate until he died, with a liver the size of a horse's, as curled up around the edges as if it had been cooked; Booth's idiocy had to burst out; the feelings the whore Alberta had toward her customers would be revealed; the dream of *stasis* could only . . . *only*, had no other possible way to go, ever, from its birth was doomed by its inflexibility . . . stagnate.

And when the stench became unbearable, a new order would come, and make new dreams and institutions, because the dream would always be there, one way or the other.

II

CUNNINGHAMS

In the uncertain season between late winter and early spring of that year it rained without letup in Eunola for nineteen straight days. Night and day, heavy, splashing drops. In that time, yards were turned into small lakes and houses were isolated from one another like stones on a field. Dampness crept inside, mildewing shoes, swelling windows and joints to cranky stiffness, and rain drenched every newly planted spring garden, washing out sprouted seeds, slim stalks, thready roots, floating topsoil away. It was a crucial season: farmers sat in kitchens and on back porches drinking coffee, waiting it out. Drains were full, ditches overflowing; children rowed boats through glassy intersections, as above them, traffic lights dumbly switched. The sound of rain falling became a daily rhythm which after a while went almost unnoticed, as life itself came to dwell inside the notion of its tock-tocks. Minds became soggy; people stood at windows watching water slide down glass in great running sheets, saying nothing, thinking nothing, only watching, absorbed, removed from anything beyond the glass and the rain.

Water had always been a factor in Eunola; it moved slow there. With the land so flat, rain simply stood when it came, and having nowhere to go, eventually, instead of running off, was either absorbed into the ground, or evaporated to become the air they breathed . . . one way or the other staying. Which was not new to the inhabitants or the land itself, because water was a constant and made the land what it was. From ocean bottom, little more than three thousand years before . . . late, as history measures . . . to river bottom when the ocean drained off, the land, as the river in its time also narrowed within new ridges and rolled south to join the ocean, became blessed with what was left behind . . . priceless garbage, precious silt, clay, minerals, sand. And whenever the river flooded . . . and with the land there so flat and so little above the level of the river bottom, the flooding then, before the levees, was often . . . the water stood again, and receding again, left behind still more deposits and then went on until, eventually, from all that standing and receding and leaving behind, a particularly felicitous patch of earth was created, a triangular basin, black with richness, alive with fertility; alluvial soil, in which if you stood long enough, it was said, your feet would take root. (This inherent dispensation from natural hardships in the earth eventually was transferred to people as well . . . generating a notion of inherent grace, qualities genetically received and transmitted . . . an inborn blessedness.)

People moved with less urgency in such fertile, watery country. Accustomed to tedium . . . waiting for natural beneficence . . . those who came—seeing how dreams could be more easily realized there—learned to sit in one place and, watching rain run down a glass, to move with time instead of against it, to wait it out, figuring in that way to hold on to what they had, in the long run. And those who came to that rich triangular-shaped patch of earth early in life and stayed did not in their old age accumulate the hard craggy faces and coiled protective stance of hill-dwellers or the worn-out hopeless look of dust-watchers, but wrinkled softly, in great folds, their bodies moving ever closer groundward, like a candle growing fat toward its bottom, melting. Because time in such a fertile place was friendly, people there had little notion of its obstinacy but, enjoying its excess, came to indulge what ease of mind was granted, those margins, in attention paid to dreams—of baton twirlers and knights-in-armor and received grace—and valued, more than accomplishment, style. Manners, method, not what you did but *how:* that was what counted and helped make footprints for them to step into.

For instance, the drinking, which in Eunola was commonly done, especially in country club circles among those considered to be the town's civic and social heart. Drinking was accepted in Eunola, being an old established ritual which helped create a sense of community and bring people together. It made for brighter gatherings, took up slack, and gave to them a world of even greater possibilities than they already had dreamed of. This was a ritual hardly ever commented upon, only practiced and perpetuated, except when its etiquette was so blatantly ignored and its style so outrageously corrupted that certain notice was not only called for, but as self-protection, demanded. Word got around fast in such a case, once it was discovered, and the transgressor pointedly identified. Certain comments were made. And made. There was one person, at the time Lolly was twirling, of whom this was true; in fact, the way she did her . . . a word never spoken unless it was done incorrectly . . . was so inappropriate that almost all they—those country clubbers —ever did say of her was that she . . . the word . . . *drank*. Anytime her name was brought up, you might as well expect the description, it was coming; either *drinks* or *has a drinking problem*.

Lady Cunningham, it was said in such carefully honed whispers that the message was never lost on the rankest stranger, *drinks*, and that was all, that was the heart of her as far as the town was concerned. Not that she did it—they did too—but *how*, which in this style-conscious place caused her to be open to contempt and left others free to sum her up brusquely with that one phrase. This, when many of them drank in great enough quantities and ruined their lives to such an extent that they might be said by any but the loosest standards to have a drinking problem; nevertheless, hers alone was singled out, hers the only problem admitted, she of all the drinkers in town the only one who *drank*, in that unmistakable tone of voice. (While her late brother-in-law, the legendary Graham, was laughingly referred to as the greatest of all town drunks but had never been said to *drink*, in that way.)

Lady Cunningham, during that unusually wet spring in Eunola, was even more isolated within glass and water than others. Having made her own, sweeter sphere of leveled-out space and time, outside the measurements of clocks and calendars, she hardly took notice of weather at all, or how long anything, rain, sun, days or nights, went on . . . but every day managed to erase dots between numbers, lines marking the end of one day, the beginning of another, so that she

would not recognize the accumulation and boxing of time or
notice how long it had gone on or feel compelled to count or
measure at all. Spending her days in a dark room with
closed curtains, Lady knew it was still raining only when
her servant Serenthea said so or when Preston spoke of it—as
he did now—at the dinner table. (To which she insisted on
coming nightly, drunk, hungry or not; it was the only rung
left.) Even so, news of weather passed over her. His voice
came and went . . . *rain,* he said . . . *crops* . . . *time to
plant* . . . it was only when he spoke of Carroll, their son
away at school, that she felt the prick of reality, the urge of
time. Lady Cunningham's eye twitched at the mention of
his name. Carroll . . .

In full, Sexton Carroll Beall Cunningham, after his great-
grandfather Sexton on the Cunningham side and his grandfather Carroll on Lady's, the Beall, side. The boy, however,
had always been called Carroll. Lady named him Sexton
only because she felt some obligation to; after all, Sexton had
established the Cunningham name in Eunola, and her son
was to be the only namesake he would produce. But once
the name was acknowledged and the obligation satisfied,
Lady left it alone, the legacy was ignored and the name
unspoken. For Lady had no use for Sexton or his history, especially the way his life ended, in such disgrace, and with
that ridiculous statue for a gravestone to boot . . . it was all
in all a bad joke to Lady. Poor dead Sexton. Who had
worked so hard. He would never in his life have believed
that his name would come to that—and in the only Cunningham family left in Eunola too—something to be thrown
in and ignored, after he had struggled so to make it respectable too and against all odds had succeeded, by dint of
sheer hard work and a creative, speculative imagination.

Sexton had come to Eunola from Cincinnati after what was called the War Between the States by those who started it and the Civil War by those who retaliated, looking, as many others were, for opportunity, as well as a new and more honorable past. But Sexton took a longer time than most scoping out the lay of the land, recognizing right away, as he was so talented in doing, that in such a familied place a man had to be careful before taking sides; a man couldn't just jump one way or another; he had to take some time first, and choose his friends and politics with a great deal of caution and forethought. And so he set out to find which people it would profit him most in the long run to become friends with and which, according to his best calculations it would not. This was the kind of thing Sexton had an uncanny knack for, for figuring out in advance how things would eventually turn out and who, after all the commotion, would finally be in control and who he should then latch on to, to begin with. A born gambler, he had a nose adept at sniffing out winners. Deciding after much concentrated study that the North's idealism and self-righteousness were less hardy than the Southern planters' intransigence, he set about doing what he could to throw in with the latter, and to make himself accessible to them. He became a liaison between the rules the Northerners set down and the needs of the Southerners . . . managing to appear sympathetic to the Union when he needed to, then going secretly from one plantation to another telling proprietors there what was happening; meanwhile as well gathering support for himself and spreading assurances as he went that he was in truth on whoever's side it profited him to seem to be on. Through little-understood and much-neglected clauses, he saw to it that the original owners kept their valuable land; he swept away un-

wanted ballot boxes; and in return asked only for small
payments, not money, never money, only a small piece of
land here from this man, another there from that one, until
before anyone realized it—because he deliberately made the
requests far enough apart that no one made the connections
—he had acquired a small empire as well as a recognizable
name: Sexton Cunningham was a known institution across
the board, a man of the people representing whichever people he chose to at any particular time. He wrangled an ap-
pointment from the government as head of Eunola's Freed-
man's Bureau, assuring the planters it was only to give him a
better vantage point from which to operate. When a
mayoral election was finally held, Sexton was where he
needed to be, available, acceptable to all, ready as ripe fruit
for picking. To no one's surprise, he was overwhelmingly
elected. For Sexton had a gift he well knew how to exploit:
he could make anybody believe, at least for a while, that he
understood that person's individual needs and problems,
and there was no voter on any side of any issue who hadn't
been convinced that Sexton when elected would act in consideration of *his* interests and for his benefit. From election
to re-election, Sexton served as mayor from 1866 until 1900.
By then he had married and buried a respected local school-
teacher, Corrie Ann Pritcher, had had the first public school
and library built and named for himself, had hired some of
the best hands in the area to produce his cotton crops, had
had a new courthouse and post office built, had raised a
daughter and son, and was the grandfather of two boys with
another on the way. In only thirty-four years, he had established his name and position, had got his land and made his
mark in Eunola's history, in a place where any kind of usur-
pation of granted privilege and grace was altogether abnor-

mal. But then it was an abnormal time and Sexton startled
them by coming up on a blind side they had not had before
that time or since, and the rooting of the Cunningham name
was without doubt his finest accomplishment . . . one which
even Lady could not help giving its due, much as she disliked the clamor surrounding his gain.

But, in time, things began to change again, and as the
heavy hand of the North began to lift, people started
breathing easier, and going back to thinking the way they
had before the war started, looking to the same people as
before to be their leaders. And before Sexton died, with the
other opportunists either broke or imprisoned or gone on to
some other gold field, and the northern politicians' interest
as pale as he had predicted it would be, new alignments
were being made. The people didn't need him as much as
they did bankers, railroad men, businessmen, and lawyers,
and now that his usefulness had run out, they could afford to resent the way he had maneuvered himself into the
town's memories and accountings of itself, meanwhile brib-
ing them out of their land. And then there was the *Cause*—
the war—which people now used and misused to their own
profit and vanity. Sexton hadn't participated. What was he
doing running their town?

The thing was, the planter was coming back into his own.
For a while, it looked as though the war was going to make
a lot of changes . . . and it did make some, some . . . but
little by little the old balance was returning, and then it
tilted, weighted against change, as it had been from the beginning.

And so in 1900 as the ground shifted this way and that,
and Sexton found he could not move fast enough to keep a
foothold, there came a time when he simply lost his sense of

direction entirely and could no longer calculate accurately about what they wanted to hear exactly, which bent of the truth it suited them to have uttered. While he perceived their state of mind correctly and was correct in thinking that not only had their tolerance for scalawags and freed slaves and their own enforced martyrdom come to an end, but that they now felt even more strongly united against the upgrading of those people who had been their slaves than they had ever felt before the war, though he was absolutely on target in believing all that, what he misunderstood was what they intended doing about all this . . . and *how* they would go about it. He didn't realize the length to which people valuing manners and gentility would go to enforce a condition like slavery, or in the new post-war world, as it was called, "Jim Crow," and yet preserve their own sweet style. How they could on the one hand make it work and on the other, never speak of the harsh things done in the name of that enforcement in anything resembling a harsh manner. He didn't understand the power of a conspiratorial silence about such things. That they would cover themselves up in a cloak of utter quiet, and communicate by means of high-signs and bywords and undecipherable gestures and make it work was altogether beyond the comprehension of an outsider like Sexton. And so when Sexton shouted "Tainted blood!" and "The dark evil threatening our fair daughters . . ." he saw them simply turn away. He lost them and was lost from them, and died before the voting in the 1900 election. Which was fortunate because he knew he would not win and his loss would be not only of the election but of his place as well. But Sexton died on his feet, campaigning. Screaming *"Redemption!"* to a meager courthouse-steps audience, he simply fell over the podium and was dead, guilty of choosing the wrong vocabulary, of holding on to a dead language, when his constituents had moved on.

Samuel, his son . . . by then middle-aged himself, with three sons . . . inherited that climate of disdain. Neither rejected nor accepted, a planter with no prestige, and more important, no knowledge of planting and no understanding of land and seasons at all, neither member nor outsider, Samuel lived out his ineffectual life, a lonely sullen man sitting on his front porch dreaming of what he could do to make Sexton proud of him. But Sam was stupid, and Sexton knew that from the beginning. He drooled as a baby and vomited on the table and didn't walk until he was more than two or say a word anyone could recognize until well up into his third year. Sexton thought Sam's dumbness probably contributed to his wife's early death, because her son and his didn't know his ass from a hole in the ground and never would. While Mattie Sue, the oldest, had all the brains and should have been the boy.

So when Sexton made out his will, he brought Sam in and very carefully spelled out his wishes. "You leave the land to the one who'll keep it in the family and work it, do you hear me, Sam? Do you understand? Not to the first or the last and not to the prettiest or the nicest or even godammit the smartest, just the one who'll most likely in your judgment keep it and work it. And for God's sake, Sam, don't sell it. *Do you understand, Sam?*"

Sexton beat Sam over the head with this, and Sam kept it in his mind always and did his best to carry out Sexton's instructions.

Sam's wife had been a manicurist at the Hotel Eunola barbershop; Sam found her easy to propose to. And she had quickly said yes, and came to live with him, and produced three sons, then fairly disappeared. The woman's name was Jewel but as she was tiny she was called Bit. Bit never left the Cunningham house—until she went with Mattie Sue for good, much later—but once the boys were old enough to do for themselves, Bit, for all notice taken, disappeared. She became like a forgotten piece of furniture, always there, taking up space and occasionally providing someone a place to sit for a minute or two but never given any notice, never looked at or made over in any way. Bit was there, and that was all.

Their three sons were Richard, Graham, and Preston. After serving in World War I, Richard came home to find the place in disrepair, with Samuel sulking and dreaming on the front porch, his mother in an advanced state of abstraction, and Mattie Sue tearing around like a house afire trying to whip his two younger brothers into the shape of farmers. So Richard announced his intentions: he wanted out. He would trade his share of the property for an education. Remembering Sexton's instructions, Sam thought it would be the right thing to do. And Richard went on to become a doctor and shuck his heritage. He was never heard from again, though they were told he lived well in Arkansas and had a family there. Graham, the middle son, being no kind of farmer, a person in need of connections, friends, wholeness, one unable to tolerate the social limbo his family now suffered, who wanted less than anything to be cut off from approval . . . Graham set out to shock and disappoint as many people as he could in as short a time and thereby gain some respectability. For if he did it harmlessly and within their context of right and wrong, they would love him for it and take care of him forever. All through school, Graham was the bad kid teachers enjoyed keeping after school because of his irresistible charm and flirtatious manner. And Graham was a success. He became accepted in the town and was a part of it and finally, as far as his family was concerned, moved out, as he began sleeping wherever an available bed turned up.

And so it was up to Preston, the third son. Five years younger than Graham, Preston simply went out one day—before he was sixteen years old—and began asking questions of the field hands about what to do and how it went, what was what. Against Mattie Sue's wishes, he quit school and started working like a laborer, to learn about the land. (Which he still did. To this day you could find Preston, out there, any day work was being done, sweating with the hands over every bale as if it were the last he'd see. He never vacationed—unable to imagine what he'd do all that time, just sitting around—and rarely left Eunola. A touchy man, sensitive and easily embarrassed, he worked, revered Lady, and that was all.)

Sam finally died, none too soon. He had a stroke that left his body half-paralyzed, putting it on even par with his mind, and finally died just after the flood of 1927, which devastated the area. Nobody was exactly sorry to see Sam go; no one really noticed, least of all Bit. All she knew was suddenly no one was eating the fried potatoes she cooked every night for Sam. One night she looked up and sure enough where Samuel had sat there was no one and so she stopped fixing fried potatoes, and that was about all it meant to Bit . . . who had been happy once in her life, working at the barbershop, poking at people's fingers.

Mattie Sue breathed a sigh of relief at the funeral, feeling as if she'd had cut off her back a hump she'd worn since birth; and came home and went back to the books she kept

so meticulously. Being a son who craved duties and looked
for more when there were none, Preston placed his hat over
his heart and paid his father the respect he'd been taught
was due elders and the dead, then went back to work. They
wrote Richard the news but got the letter back stamped
"Not at this Address" so no one knew if he ever heard of his
father's death. Only Graham truly grieved. Graham wept
over the bar at which he sat when they brought him the
news and wailed unashamedly at the funeral, and for weeks
afterward sobbed into his drinks. Loud and long Graham
lamented the death of his father. Until one day it was
through, the mourning was over, and Graham went back to
being a respectable town drunk; after that Samuel Cunningham's name was not mentioned by any of them. It was
as if he had been erased, as if someone had wet a finger and
smudged him out and left nothing of him but a trace, those
two worn places on the front porch where his favorite rocker
had sat. (The chair stayed there for years after his death,
slowly rotting in the damp Eunola climate, until Lady redec-
orated, had the front porch torn down, and gave the rocker
to Judge, the handyman.)

Preston got through the flood and the Depression without
suffering too great a hardship. With the help of Mattie Sue
. . . who never married but stayed at the place until Lady
came, when Preston was thirty-one . . . he hired more
hands, bought more land, and saw it produce. Truly, he
carried out Sexton's final wishes. When Preston married,
Mattie Sue and Bit, at his suggestion, were moved into a
three-story downtown house, where they lived still. The
year Lolly met James Blue, the spring it rained so much,
when Carroll Cunningham was due to return from the prestigious military academy he had been attending, Bit was

seventy-six years old and still wandering outside time in her mind. Mattie Sue, who was older, took care of her, both having been set aside to live out their lives with only Lady bothering to visit them. Or she did, before the drinking.

And so Carroll's father, Preston, earned his inheritance according to his grandfather's stipulations. He took over where Sexton left off as far as the land went if not the position, prestige, or name, which he left—along with the child—in Lady's hands . . .

They were thin now, and weak, barely able to hold the fork she lifted from her plate. Pale white hands.

In the early days, months, years of their marriage she had lain next to her plain solid husband and to the rhythm of his snores had made plans, endlessly . . . plans for the next morning, the night ahead, the day after, no farther, only just ahead, in the very next time of her life. She had to see it first, and plan what to do. Anything except face unequivocal time or stand still. There had to be diversions, something interesting to lighten boredom and use the very next time of her life. But what? It changed. She had to make plans constantly. The next few minutes and then the next . . . and when imagination failed her and she drew a sudden blank, anxiety began to close in, breath came hard . . . this was what she had to forestall . . . and a seed of panic sprouted, and sent roots deep. Empty time, such a long time, so many minutes, days, encroaching on her life, squeezing hard. No, she had to keep ahead. Nip panic before it bloomed. For if it ever surfaced, she would stand in the face of something unbearable . . . not diversions and planning but the renewable unending present: what she unquestionably was . . . and was . . . and was. It was too awful, she would not be able to bear it. Life had to be better, a constantly changing series.

What they said of her was in fact true: Lady Cunningham did drink in great quantities. All day and well up into the night, until the light went out and she was easy, in blackness. Judge bought a case of bourbon at a time and carried it in the truck past Eunola, south of town in the opposite direction from the trailer camp, out a blacktop road, onto a gravel, past the dirt side road leading to Granny Peavey's, to the Cunningham place, as ordinary a delivery as food and mail. What they said was not a lie. And yet the words themselves were not the message or what a person, having heard them uttered, came away remembering because the fact of her drinking was in this case not the point at all. That they spoke of it, and how, was the point. Opinion surrounded and overwhelmed the content of the statement, like an ornate gilt frame on a plain ordinary pencil sketch. And all you came away remembering was the frame . . . or in her case the disapproval.

The rules were, you could drink all you wanted, you could do it every night and break chairs or cry and scream or throw other people fully clothed into swimming pools in the dead of winter, you could rant and rave and sing stale songs off-key and tell the same dull jokes in the same unfunny way party after party and not be criticized for it; you could scream and accuse and discreetly seduce, you could act all the fool you wanted . . . all this was given and you were allowed great leeway as long as you (and this was the deciding factor) did it *with* them, got drunk on their terms, in a group, among them, with the others and in that way showed everyone what kind of drunk you were, how your face looked when you were farthest gone: what you did when your imagination and fancy were let loose, whether drink freed in you some wild hidden longing or simply exaggerated what was obvious. As long as you revealed where it was you in your heart of hearts dwelt, they never criticized or if they did, it was only within the context of friendship, framed by their great tolerance and bounty. But if you went into your room and drank alcohol in solitude and never let them see not only the effect the alcohol had on you . . . the tracks imbedded beneath your eyes, the scrapings alongside your mouth and down your chin . . . but the need as well, if you kept your secret possibilities to yourself, then they would say of you as they did of Lady Cunningham that you drank or that you had a drinking problem, or both. They wanted you with them and that was that; otherwise, you made a mockery of their fondest rituals and ceremonies.

Again Preston spoke of the boy. She heard his name . . . Carroll . . . Carroll . . . Now that he was coming home from school, he said, didn't she think they ought to encourage him to go to college and which did she think was best and how did she feel about buying him a car . . . him . . . Carroll. Her son. It was raining. Rain slid down the window behind Preston's ruddy bald head; sweat as if in imitation ran down his forehead, one drift replacing another . . . another . . . on and on. He always sweated. He always looked as if he were going to run himself apart any minute. On and on . . . rain . . . sweat . . .

She drifted. Things came and quickly went, leaving little behind. Nothing lasted. When she first came to Eunola, Mattie Sue and Bit were there and then had gone. For a while she and Preston went to parties, but when people started wanting her to come so badly, she had felt compelled to push them off, to shock them, by coming when she said she wasn't and staying home when she had *rsvp*'ed yes. That had been interesting for a while, but once the flamboyant behavior and outlandish clothes became dependable —once they were the expected thing—she went on to something else. She took trips. Preston wouldn't go, but she went anyway, alone or with her mother, and then suddenly stopped going. Nothing lasted, everything dissipated, especially her enthusiasms, which were fickle and apt to wane before she got past first instructions. Anticipation was all; reality disappointed. Even the birth of her son. Like the chance appearance of a close acquaintance come for a weekend, she made her house ready for his arrival and saw he was cared for, but felt no implicit urge regarding him, any more than anything else. Time drifted as she did, nothing accumulating, nothing telling her what to do or how to choose. Only the power of what she took to be her saving grace carried her, her family inheritance, that carefully taught, ingrained by now, indifference. She would keep it to the end, not knowing what price it extracted, this nonchalance, that cool aloofness, which allowed no flames to burn long. Floating above her life, never dipping a toe into it, never muddying the hem of her skirt, she remained adrift. Nights, lying awake, planned. So that she would never confront a situation she had not already known in her imagination.

And how long, she had wondered then, could she play her life that way, improvising day by day, thinking that when panic drew in on her and threatened to envelop her mind, something would always turn up to disengage her from it . . . how long?

Until she *drank*.

Then panic was eased and any spark which threatened to

subdue her valued indifference taken care of; dampened. And nothing pushed her in circles; she didn't have to think what to do next. Or hardly, to think at all.

She kept sending Carroll away, from one school to another. When Preston questioned this, she protested it was best for the child, saying she would never send a child of hers to Eunola public school or any public school for that matter. She kept him at a distance always. The spark . . .

With the rain down around his head like a lady's veil, Preston finally shut up and ate and stopped speaking of the boy . . . having been in no way encouraged by her to continue, her silence as she poked at her food plain indication that she would say nothing of how she felt about him . . . whether coming home or going to college or receiving a new car . . . and perhaps felt nothing as well.

Wiping her mouth, she excused herself from the table and, using all her reserves, managed to drift away in her usual style. Closing the door to her bedroom firmly behind her, she leaned against it. Her hair clung to the back of her neck, clammy. Rain hit against the window.

Nine o'clock. Finally. One more was almost used up.

Preston sat for a long time after she left, staring at his plate, then wiped his damp bald head with his napkin and rose, thinking of the boy. This time he would find out, he was sure. But what could *he* do? More than anything Preston wanted to hold on to what he had and keep it the same, but how? You couldn't change misfortune's course, you could only ride it out and find a way to accommodate whatever unexpected or unwanted thing came, and place it where it would go in your life. He thought there was nothing else *to* do. To his mind, he asked little of Lady; only that she accept his blind adoration, nothing less than his life

at her feet, in return for which he allowed her the indul-
gence of every eccentricity and whim, including the drinking. She was all he had, and in his need to keep her, he rec-
onciled himself to the situation at hand . . . being so little in
touch with her he wouldn't have known what to say anyway
or what alternatives to suggest . . . but he would never understand why she did it or stayed on if it was so bad she had
to be drunk to bear it. But women had their ways and Preston had never understood one, from his mother to Mattie
Sue to Lady, and because of his need to keep this one with
him, he let it go by. Though he knew he was doing her no
favor. Still, what could he do? And still go on with his work
and, most of all, not lose her?

But the boy was different. He was like her, like all the
Bealls. No telling what he'd do if he found out, and this time
he was sure to.

Preston left the table and went to his room. He would be
up early the next day . . . he always was . . . and maybe by
then the rain would have quit so he could get on with the
season's planting.

Lady's family said of Carroll from the first, "He's a Beall
through and through, I don't see a trace of Cunningham in
him." And to understand how Lady felt about that and
about Preston himself, you had to have some idea how
Bealls felt about Cunninghams in the first place, because
while to Lolly and the Peaveys and even Frank, Cunninghams were *the* Cunninghams, people at the top, as high
as you could get, Peaveys' and Lasswells' knowledge about
what went on in Eunola was limited and so far from accurate you couldn't measure by it. Because they had no idea
which families were in truth *the* families, especially since

those people were seen so rarely and their influence so un-
consciously felt. The Families lived out from the city limits
of town, in the county, often in other small towns, which
having once been only plantations now bore their family
name. The Wilson Paynes, for instance, lived in Paynes and
the Bubba Darcys in Darcy. Their children did not attend
public school for one day but were sent to academies and
prep schools and Miss Somebody-or-Other's finishing school,
or were educated at home by tutors, in which case they
would have read Sir Walter Scott, Mark Twain, Longfellow,
and Dickens by the time they were in their teens. These
Families only came into town from time to time when and
as they were needed, to nudge the people and remind them
what was what and how they should vote or what they
should do next in the best interests of the white man, decency, and the state. Which in their minds were synony-
mous. Which were their first priorities: white men, decency,
and the state. Themselves, their style, their space on earth.
Meanwhile buffaloing the poor white man into thinking that
because he was included on that exclusive list, it profited
him to stand by these other people and with them, and to do
what they suggested, in order to keep the list intact and
maintain his steady place. So that *white* would always take
priority over *poor*.

It was these people's influence that cost Sexton his election and prestige in 1900. Symbols of leadership (though
not themselves leaders, in any civic capacity; none held
offices or presided over meetings or arbitrated justice), they
were like kings and queens of a country which no longer has
need of kings or queens in the everyday working-out of its
people's lives but has a definite, time-established spiritual
need of their royal presence, the very fact of their visible
grace and nobility living proof that life offered more than

what they knew, the simplest working-out. That there was grace incarnate.

The planters kept the town moving or still as they saw fit, and mollified radicalism by keeping the rednecks and populists from taking over and turning Eunola into the kind of town you found in the hills, those insular, thick-headed communities where strangers of any color were suspect and all change considered detrimental. If Sexton had been campaigning on the courthouse steps of one of those towns, he'd have been on the right track, because they *liked* to hear what they were thinking told to them, and then wanted to hear it again; they could sit all afternoon reiterating who it was they were bitter toward and how they were going to carry out their revenge. Over in those hill towns they said everything and in a tone of voice fitting the intention too: no cloaked conspiracies. But Eunola was properly quiet and had its own sense of propriety and structure; before anybody would as much as listen to you, not to mention vote for you, you had to learn all the bywords and high signs and secret gestures, and be able to use them. Now if you said that to most Eunolites, especially somebody like a Peavey, who profited least from agreeing, they would tell you you were crazy; that they paid no attention at all to what those people said or thought. But for instance when the flood of '27 came and wiped out their homes and crops and many of their lives, and they had to look to someone to lead them collectively to high ground and see that they did not starve or drown, the responsibility was quickly handed to a Payne, the present Wilson Payne III's father, Wilson Payne, Jr. When it came down to it, they listened all right and the word was passed on, and they did what it was very genteelly suggested they do, because they left up to those peo-

ple the decisions as to what was best for them . . . in the interests of the white man, decency, and the state. It was
another dream of theirs. And so civic and social leaders, im-
potent to use their positions, created their own community
by drinking together.

Now Beall was an old Memphis name and to Bealls . . .
and planters like the Paynes . . . Cunninghams were still
newcomers, usurpers who had got what they had by scan-
dalously taking advantage of the reverses of other, better
people, a circumstance they could partially correct through
the institution Preston used, marriage, but even then not entirely.

Lady Beall was Cotton Carnival Queen in 1930. At the
time, Preston was in Memphis bargaining with cotton brokers, and because of the carnival, which he had not known
about, could not find a hotel room. Carroll Beall—a cotton
man—invited Preston out to have dinner at his house and to
spend the night and stay for the festivities over the weekend. Preston, already thirty-one, had not stopped working
long enough to think of marriage before, but when he laid
eyes on Lady . . . blond and pale and cool . . . he thought
she was the most beautiful creature he had ever seen, and
with the same natural doggedness that enabled him to go
out in the field and take over the farm, pursued her. He
would not take no for an answer. Weekend after weekend
he came to Memphis. Carroll Beall thought Preston a good
man but no match for the wit and guile of Lady. But then,
Lady made sure no one could ever predict what she was
going to do next, and one way to keep her diversions going
and her life from winding down to where she would have to
look too closely at it, was to grab for the unexpected . . .
whatever came by, to reach for it. That way she could hold

on to her indifference and never feel responsible. "I never make decisions," she often said of herself. "I only *do*."

And so one morning when she said she was going to Eunola, Carroll Beall figured it was just another of her crazy larks. (Lady's mother, however, took it more seriously. After hearing the news, she swallowed three more pills, lay longer in her dark room, professed another illness.)

After she married Preston, Lady found to her own amazement she could not leave, had no talent for it. Though the marriage was meaningless and there was little for her in Eunola, nothing else offered itself with such appeal and urgency that she could up and go for it, whatever the consequences, as she had with Preston. When Carroll was born, Lady's mother sent Serenthea—the black lady who had raised Lady—to Eunola. She was now Lady's only friend. Lady simply could not leave, not having that gift.

And so from both parents their son Carroll inherited tenacity. He had the doggedness of Preston, tempered with the natural inborn aloofness inherent in Bealls . . . the conviction Lolly longed for, that they had no need to prove anything to anyone, that their life itself was proof of their worth and that they need not exert an ounce of energy justifying it, it being its own explanation. This cooled the doggedness and gave him room to maneuver; to place it at will. And from Sexton he inherited a hardheaded money-making turn of mind, encouraged by his being cut off from his family all these years, off at school, unfettered by scruple or tradition.

This was the boy coming home.

One night the rain stopped. It did not ease off but just

quit—like that—in the early hours of a morning, when few were up to witness. The sudden quiet, however, soon caused a general awakening all over town as people sat up in their beds, not immediately certain what had happened to make everything seem so different. (Frank Lasswell, however, attuned to signs, knew instantly and went outside to see.)

The next morning the air was so hot and still and wet even birds' songs seemed labored, struggling to get through. A pall of moisture lay across the flat rich earth, mosquitoes swarmed, and the sun, wrapped up in wetness, looked altogether dissipated, like a used soggy cotton ball. The water held, flat and solemn, as the earth waited for the return of some dryness, when the planting would begin.

Lady slept on, her gray silk draperies shutting out all indications of time and weather stopped or continuing. When she wakened, her face buried in pillows, one arm hanging to the floor like a peeled broken limb, she thought immediately of Carroll—soon, only weeks now—and, trembling, called for Serenthea.

III

THE RIVER

While Main Street came to an abrupt stop at the levee, Court did not but crossed River Road and ascended it; you could drive up the levee there and then turn left and go across it for one long block, or even drive straight down to the edge of the water itself. Your car rumbled and shook when you did, as it took the ridges and bumps of the old stone blocks that went from Court south to Jefferson and continued far beneath the water's surface.

Winter to the north had been fierce that year, and spring unusually wet. Now the water was halfway up the stone blocks, much farther than usual, and out in it, island trees were so immersed all you could see were the very tops, like fingertips reaching for help. Eunolites came to see; they couldn't remember when the water had been so high. And because the river ran straight through the heart of the country, from northern border to southern rim, people watching it became worried, especially those along the lower sections of its course. Because even though methods of flood control were sophisticated now and the levee continued the whole way . . . still, there was only so much you could do. Especially since it wasn't just this one river you had to consider, but all those it served to drain as well. Like twigs running to branches and then to a trunk and roots, lesser rivers from north and east and west all rushed to one destination, pouring down to relieve their excess as mountain snows joined rivers and came through hill country and on down to flat, and all ran and gathered, small ones connecting to larger, and those to even larger still, all coming finally to this one great and dependable support, the center trunk, running down the heart of the country, serving to drain the rest. The river was much on people's minds that spring. Especially in that flat land near the river's mouth, which, being so full by the time it got there, the river particularly endangered. And Eunola, being only some two hundred miles from the ocean and so flat, was one of the towns that might have been threatened.

But wasn't. Not any more. Although the town had once been situated in a particularly sharp elbow of the river, so that anytime it rose at all the town was in danger and its downtown threatened, that was no longer true. Government engineers had come after the '27 and another less severe flood and suggested a way to deflect that violence and make the town safer. A local congressman in fact made a name for himself by securing funds to have it done. Now the water that lay immediately to Eunola's west, on the other side of the levee downtown, was not actually the river itself but a quiet lake only fed by the river, a placid comma made by the giant's erratic hand; a prosperous slackwater port which drew barges from up and down the river and even from

other parts of the world; a resting place. Its northern chan-
nel having been cut off, the river now went straight south
instead of making that jagged, inhospitable visit to Eunola's
west flank.

Standing on the levee, at the crest of the paved section between Court and Jefferson Streets, if you looked straight
ahead, west, you saw—just past the pleasure boats and
barges and the Yacht Club harbored there—an island of
trees in the middle of the lake, no good for anything, all
mud and underbrush and wild things; more water; the horizon. To the right, north, the lake curved and lay flat and was
calm. As vacation homes abounded along that bank, small
fishing boats usually hugged the tree-lined shore and cabin
cruisers and outboard motor boats cut through the deeper
sections. But not to the south. There, violence still threatened and pulled. And standing on the levee, if the sun was
bright and you concentrated, you could sometimes catch a
glimpse of something silver in that direction—far away,
nothing real, only a shine, a gesture—its brightness thrown
off in all directions, reflected not only in the sunlight itself
but in the water too, where its mirror image lay next to that
of the sun's, illuminating rolls and currents and making the
water come alive. So much light down there, bouncing back
and forth. You couldn't always see it, but when the day and
the light were perfect, you could, and you knew the water
the silver was being reflected in was not the quiet lake before you but its more powerful source, pulling south, moving, urgent, headed implacably for its emptying, nature's
stronger argument, the river itself. The bright sparkling silver shine came from the bridge, the only one that crossed
the river for a hundred miles: it led to the next state, west.
It was a beautiful thing, that silver shine; it made you want

to drive out and see its source, find out what could sparkle so.

Otherwise, you couldn't actually tell from the levee where the lake stopped and the river began because water went on and on without noticeable borders or defining lines to indicate where one ended and the other began. (But if you were in a boat and accidentally went out into it, there was no doubt, the border was unmistakable and exact . . . the instant you hit the river and felt its pull you knew where you were all right, without looking for a drawn line.) From the levee, however, it was all—simply—water. The only thing you could actually see indicating otherwise was, sometimes, that magnificent gesture of shining silver, announcing that the river was still there, not far.

The lake itself was quiet. A resting place away from the river's fickle violence. A place for fishing and water skiing and play, with inviting sand bars speckled about, suitable shores for picnics and swimming. Fed by the river, immune to its worst and most arbitrary bullying, no one in Eunola had to worry so much about the river any more. *It* accommodated *them*.

IV

GRANNY

Death never occurred to the old woman. Its specter did not accompany her old age, the fear of it was not a factor in her life; the older she got the less attention she seemed to pay it and the less likely she seemed to expect it in her case though she certainly knew it was naturally getting closer. But this one had her eye too keenly on something else: survival. As cagey as a cur, as patient as a buzzard, she held on to it like a tick to a dog. Stolidly she sat and let the others of her family scurry about satisfying her needs. Ruthlessly she reached out and scavenged their lives, picking at their fears, gnawing on their uncertainties, nibbling at their futures, keeping a firm clawlike grip on their undiminishing guilt. *Whatever it takes to get it* was her motto; expedience, the basis of her resourcefulness. And if what it took was gobbling her offspring, like a caged hamster mother with nothing better to do . . . well, the old woman could handle that with ease, she could wolf one down for breakfast and blithely pick her teeth at lunch, with only a belch at dinnertime to remind her.

She lived alone now . . . deserted, she called it, even by her husband Matthew, not two months after the last child—Felton—married and left. Matthew Peavey didn't walk out, however . . . knowing she'd have found him wherever he went, having no place to go . . . he went the only way he knew of that was safe and would protect him from everyone, even her, and Martha Moseley Peavey was not for a minute fooled by the coroner's report. "Coward," she growled. "Up and died as soon as the last one left. Tight-assed coward." Matthew Peavey might have done that too; might have looked at his alternatives, and reckoning confrontation with the unknown a prospect perhaps less formidable than that of living alone with his wife, might have taken that gamble, might have as she said, just up and died to avoid testing the odds. Matthew was a loyal man, a carpenter, and not one to skirt his duty. Still . . . living with Martha might have been asking one more battle than he, and he a Peavey, was up to. His children buried him with the utmost understanding of his decision.

And so Granny Peavey stayed on in spite and resentment at the house where all her kids had been born and grew up. Though it was just a shack, small and rundown, Bo and Felton and Esker, her sons, painted it white every spring to keep it looking decent even though out where it was, square in the middle of Preston Cunningham's cotton field, nobody but family and pickers and Preston ever saw it anyway. It was located south of Eunola, toward Cunninghams'. Before you got to their house, you went down a dirt road barely wide enough for a car or truck to turn onto and just rutted and grooved enough to about decimate the shocks of any

that did; right before the old rundown cemetery no longer
used for burying was Granny's place.

"Spite," Zhena, the middle daughter, said. "Just because
she knows how hard it is for us to get out there, that's why
she stays. And with no telephone. So we'll have to *prove*
she's still important to us. If you ask me, it's pure spite."

Actually they perpetuated Granny Peavey's survival plan
with little encouragement or need for inducement from her.
After all, she had been laying the groundwork all their lives
and now, scared witless of her, they fawned about like flies,
and she hardly had to lift a hand or utter a sound to keep
things moving. For instance, Granny never said they had
to bring her any food. She never even said she had the
need. All she did was mention . . . quietly, offhandedly . . .
that she was no longer cooking and the only pot she put on
the stove any more was a coffeepot and that once a day and
she guessed she'd just have to get by from now on on that
and the measly crop of peas she harvested from her garden.
She just slyly let that slip to each daughter one by one and
pretty soon they were gathering together deciding who
would take hot meals to Granny on which days and who
would bring the staples in between. So much for food. Without ever coming right out and saying. Then there was the
garbage . . . Granny thought sons ought to handle garbage,
which being the case it would take more drastic measures
than offhanded remarks, sons' guilt being tougher to get
hold of, but in the long run, the longest lasting. She started
pitching things out the back door. Cans, rotted meat, stale
cake, used tissues, eggshells, mats of hair, torn socks, syrup
bottles . . . and never said a word about it, just made sure
each son when he came out went to the back door and saw
it. And soon after, the boys arranged that schedule too, with

Bo and Esker and Felton alternating weeks to come out and make a haul to the dump, wondering what might be next on her never-ending agenda.

Granny knew exactly what she was doing. She just let them stew in their own juices until she got what she needed.

The day of Matthew's funeral, Granny had Felton drive her downtown after the ceremony and without telling him where they were going or why, directed him with grunts and points, first to the Post Office, which she came out of with a sheaf of papers and forms, and then down the street to Solomon's Department Store, where she stayed it seemed to Felton an awfully long time; then back home again. (Felton never asked why. He only took her where she wanted to go. Felton knew what he was doing, too.) That was the last time Granny Peavey was seen in town until Lolly's last performance as a twirler eighteen years later.

Her children were also afraid that if she didn't have enough out where she lived and had to come to their houses for it, she might never leave and they'd be stuck with her. Not knowing in what disdain she held all of them, so taken up with clothes for the children and PTA, with getting to church and buying, buying, buying; so pitifully small-minded, such a diminishment from her to them. Where was the rage . . . the gall . . . the nerve? With too much Peavey, she said, and not enough Moseley in their blood, they squalled and mewled worse than her pups. TV sets they had to have, washing machines, new cars, corduroy jackets, dining room suites, fitted sheets . . . trying to get what everybody else had, it was degrading. But she never let any of them know how farfetched it was that she would ever deign sleep in their too-soft beds because that particular fear was one of her finest tools.

They brought scraps for her dogs, washing powder, bread, coffee cakes, pies, cornbread ("Have you ever seen her eat?" Johnnie Ruth asked Zhena once. "I think she feeds half what we bring her to those blamed dogs!"), and bars of soap, enough soap to bathe all Eunola. This never ceased to amaze Granny. It was true she stank and she knew that was why they brought it, but the soap bars didn't do anything to alter her smell. Couldn't. Because she never unwrapped them. She had stacks in the bathroom closet where towels were meant to be, one hundred twenty-eight at last count, most of which were—because it was cheapest and plainest— Ivory. There were so many bars of Ivory she kept them on a shelf to themselves, like precious collectors' items. So that when the bathroom closet was opened, you saw wavy stripes of blue and white going up and down that shelf, with "It floats," "It floats," "It floats," in red, over and over, and "99 44/100% Pure" right beside "It floats" the same number of times. Granny snorted when they laid more soap in front of her; she never bathed and didn't intend to start. She only "ragged off" as she called it at the sink once a week. Sitting in water made her feel ridiculous; it took away her edge and made her soft. They could do it; she'd be damned if she would just because they brought her so much soap. But she never told them to stop and so they kept bringing it and she kept stacking it and building her private collection.

Granny made a decent income for herself, and if she hadn't been so insistent about keeping her children in tow, she could have supported herself without any help, what with Matthew's Social Security coming in and her having a good job and the house being paid for.

The day she went to Solomon's she and Zach drew up a stiff contract. For doilies. As long as the demand held,

Granny would crochet doilies, three to a set, which Zach Solomon would have exclusive right to sell. And Granny had on the spot devised terms that would increase the value of her work and the payment she would receive if and as the demand for them grew . . . which it did. Zach was constantly after her to make more, they were that much in demand, because they were that beautiful. Intricate, lacy things, as light and delicate as cobwebs, as fragile and weightless as Granny was durable. No one else made doilies so beautiful, yet watching Granny work, it was amazing that they turned out at all. Bent down so far her head seemed about to tumble in her lap, she whispered curses as she worked, her thick stumpy fingers, swollen, crooked, and brown, moving wildly, quickly, furiously. With her crochet hook going like a sword, she seemed to be stabbing at the work instead of weaving it. And yet as her fingers poked and ran, a pattern began to emerge, spun from the threads she so hatefully married. Flowers appeared and fragile lacework, tiny moons and stars, intertwining vines, patterns of fleur-de-lis, swirls and circles, tiny knotted rosebuds, wispy lacelike leaves. Crocheted with fingers of rage, products of her fury, the doilies were wrought madly in feverish fits when she sat in her rocker and produced as many as sixteen in one day. And when the passion and rage in her reached its zenith she howled out loud, bayed and roared to the cotton field, weaving at the same time rosebuds and moons and baby's breath. With no one to hear but her dogs . . . and the rats and crickets and long long dead of that rundown old cemetery close by.

People were always dumping unwanted puppies on the gravel road which ran about a mile from her house and led

on to the Cunningham place, and the pups drifted down to
the dirt road and through the cotton field up to Granny
Peavey's, where they mated, increased, and thrived. For
nourishment, they ate scraps she threw out and hunted for
birds and squirrels and possum, and all in all, if a pup was
strong, that was enough to keep him going. If he was not, he
died; that was how it went. And when their mistress went
into one of her fits of howling, once the dogs got used to it,
hardly a head was lifted among them. Some, when they first
arrived, cocked an ear and lifted a lid in wonderment, but
upon seeing their elders' dispassion, learned to imitate it;
soon they were, like the others, sleeping right through. In
fact, the prime purpose in those dogs' lives seemed to be to
get back to sleep. Sometimes they'd get up and walk around,
lick Granny's feet, sniff the ground, yawn, stretch, scratch,
turn in circles, look at the sky, snap at a flea, bite at a tick,
but all of it was done for one reason only and that was to get
easier; to find a new place to curl; to make themselves more
comfortable . . . in order to get back to sleep. Even eating
seemed an interruption they could hardly wait to finish.
One time Esker tried to count how many dogs Granny had,
and got up to twenty-seven before realizing he'd counted an
active one more than once and had skipped a bitch's sucking
pups, so the count wasn't too accurate.

There was only one person who agreed with Granny Peavey about the overall stupidity of both Eunolites and her
own children and that was Frank Lasswell, toward whom
because of that agreement and unspoken understanding,
Granny directed a particularly deep and bitter hatred. He
knew too much, had too little guilt, and was on to her tricks
too much to suit Granny.

It was early spring when Lolly first brought James Blue out to Granny's house. Lolly got on well with Granny, mainly because she wasn't afraid of her and didn't kowtow to her . . . she knew how to flatter her without investing much of herself in the bargain. And whether it was Granny's dislike for Frank or simply boredom, or her mischievous nature or affection for Lolly, was hard to say . . . but once Lolly started bringing James Blue out to her grandmother's house, Granny encouraged the young couple to keep coming, knowing full well they were meeting in secret and were bound for trouble, going to that old cemetery.

"It's a strange place for a cemetery" was James Blue's first remark on seeing it, and it certainly was, though when it was first built, during Sexton Cunningham's term as mayor, the site seemed appropriate enough. People thought Eunola would move that way, south down the river instead of east away from it, and when in 1880 Sexton proposed that the graveyard be fenced off there, nobody much objected; anyway they were still listening to Sexton then, and thinking he knew what was what. There were other vestiges of old Cunningham's wrongheadedness. An abandoned clapboard church whose bell still rang in the wind, a vacant store with cylindrical red gas pumps rusting in front, here and there the beginnings of a house, or the leavings . . . a chimney . . . from a fire. But almost all the land in that direction was used for planting now. Being in the river basin, it was rich and fertile and more valuable to plant than live on: acres and acres plowed, turned, and planted, almost exclusively in cotton . . . as stubborn a dream as the other and as likely to fail because of its intransigence. Matthew had bought the land when out there was going to be town and because it was so close to the cemetery the three acres had been cheap.

Since Matthew's death, Preston Cunningham time and again
had tried to buy Granny Peavey out, offering her all kinds of
prices, which she consistently refused. Everybody else had
sold and Matthew might have too if he'd lived, but Mrs.
Peavey said she never would.

And so there were two square plots of land in that entire
part of the county that were not being cultivated and made
to turn, if not a profit, at least an exchange product for
money: Granny Peavey's and the cemetery.

"I'll be here," she vowed, "as long as Sexton Cunningham
is." Sexton's body lay beneath the big live oak which spread
itself throughout almost the entire perimeter of the graveyard.

When Lolly came off the football field Homecoming
night, she was flushed and radiant in her triumph; blood
was still in her head. She had outshone the queen and her
rhinestone crown, had outdone them all, and easily. The
handstands, as she glittered right side up then upside down,
again and again all the way off the field, her gold sequins
battling reflections with the field lights, had been a last-
minute inspiration the band director scolded her for. It was,
he had said afterward, unfair of her to do something un-
planned like that; it had thrown the rest of the halftime show
off-schedule and caused the returning football players to interrupt coronation ceremonies and make everyone feel awk-
ward. The truth was, though she didn't say it, it was the
crowd that threw the show off, not Lolly. Their screams had
grown to a peak of hysteria as she finished her act and
turned like a ferris wheel off the field. It took them one step
too far and the queen was crowned in the rush of that hysteria, which was only encouraged by the players' untimely entrance. There was so much milling about and mumbling and

yelling you could hardly hear the Coronation March. But the queen smiled as though she didn't notice, and only later broke down; she could have killed Lolly that night, she said, and so could her mother.

Coming up from the last handstand, she had seen her war memorial air force lieutenant waiting at the fence with her father, sipping coffee and watching her. He had smiled and tipped his hat, just as he did during parades, and Lolly looked from him to Frank, puzzled, wondering what they'd said to one another. It was the first time she had seen him without his silver glasses. His eyes, as she had expected, were a high solid blue that almost put her off, it was so intense.

Lolly never stayed for the last half of a game. She cared nothing for football and never went to dances afterward, not even to the Homecoming Dance, which would be a big formal affair lasting most of the night. She and Frank would go home after the halftime show as always.

"Lolly, this is Lieutenant James Blue . . ." Frank was saying, and Lolly, with the blood in her head just beginning to trickle back in place, inwardly soared. It was the first time in her life she had been excited by the presence of a single other person. Crowds she knew about . . . but this, this was something else. And straight off she lied to Frank by pretending to see Blue for the first time. Frank never knew about the silver wings or Cecil Cyril DeLoach or the sunglasses, because Lolly met Blue as if they were strangers, and her slight smile and quick nod and faint "Hello, nice to meet you" gave him no clue. As for Lolly, she had never lied to Frank before and if she had thought of it would not have dreamed she could do it so easily. But there, it was done before she knew it, it didn't hurt at all, and from that moment

on she and Blue were in conspiracy against her father, a fact
which encouraged Blue enormously because he of course
saw it all.

It was spring. The long siege of rain had lifted and the
land, after a week of dry weather, had become friable
enough to turn. Planting was to begin that week. It was the
first time Lolly had brought Blue to Granny's house and
when the two of them left to go to what Lolly said was a secret place, Blue noticed a look of childish glee pass from
Lolly to her grandmother.

The night was pleasantly cool. Out there, the land was so
uninterruptedly flat you could see in a full circle where the
earth touched the edge of the sky. It was as if a black bowl
dotted with bits of clear glass had been turned upside down
over the earth and you were caught in the middle of it underneath the bowl, the way that sky surrounded you all
around to the farthest edge of your vision.

"Just keep on going down the dirt road," Lolly said.

The lights of James's car showed little ahead but road,
which vanished into darkness. On either side he could make
out land being turned, tilled, prepared for planting, rows
which went on and on until he couldn't see them any more.
He thought they were going into a darkness there was no
end to, where if they needed it, no help could be depended
on to appear. The farther he drove into it, the more helpless
he felt; he seemed to be shedding customary protections like
layers of clothing . . . assumptions which in the middle of
darkness didn't count for anything. It was like being in a
place where a language different from your own was spoken, with people all around busy, scurrying about while you

stood needing help, pleading in a language no one understood. The ruts in the road were deep and too frequent to avoid, and the two of them bounced their heads on the car's roof as they went on, and the steering wheel jerked back and forth in his hands. James turned his lights up from dim to bright and pretty soon saw straight ahead of him, in the middle of the road, looming high up over his car, like the entrance to some other world, iron gates.

"What the . . . ?"

"Just keep going." Lolly giggled.

The gates were huge, about ten feet tall, and on either side of them he could make out the beginnings of a spiked iron fence. James squinted and frowned, trying to make some sense of it, as each thing became revealed to him and the lights took in what was ahead. The road ended at the gates. Simply came to a stop there; there was nowhere else to go, unless you wanted to take off out into the cotton field. There was an arc over the gate formed by two iron rods, and between them, in iron letters welded separately in place: "EUNOLA EST. 1880." Beyond the fence he saw . . . at first he wasn't sure because it seemed so unlikely but then what would be likely where he was? . . . but, closer, he saw that it was what he suspected . . . and that's when he said what he did about it being a strange place for a cemetery.

"The Dead End," Lolly said, giggling again. And she told him how the graveyard had been built there and how when the rest of the land had been turned into a cotton field nobody had had the nerve to move the bodies and so it had stayed. At the end of a road in the middle of a cotton field beyond Granny Peavey's.

James cut his motor but left on his lights. Cricket music, like shrill vibrating metal, throbbed in his ears.

The gravestones, small and cracked, tilting this way and that, leaned in toward one another, and clumps of weeds reached up around the base of each one and obscured the inscriptions. Most of the stones were simply straight markers, small and rounded at the top, but James could make out at least one that was different, a lichen-covered angel which stood with wings outspread, one half chipped away. Its neck had broken, and the head dangled to one side, held by an iron cable. The angel was just past the trunk of the oak.

The tree grew from what seemed to be the exact center of the graveyard. It was enormous, draped in Spanish moss like a dancer sporting a feather boa. Its trunk branched out low, reaching and stretching in all directions, each large branch giving way to many more smaller ones, one after the other, until the tip ends finally grazed the ground. It hung heavily over the graves as if in protection, like a mama fowl daintily settling a feather skirt over her brood. And beneath, roots foraged through the ground, nosing this way and that, tunneling over the years and finally coming to curl around the boxes planted there.

Moonlight filtered down through the thick gnarled branches and small leaves, and made each gravestone look whiter than it actually was. The tree seemed the oldest thing James Blue had ever seen . . . its thick trunk so steady, its tiny leaves trembling as if fear moved through them, a contradiction in itself.

Lolly was getting out of the car, urging him to follow.

"And turn out the lights."

She went over the fence next to the gates.

He was afraid of falling on the sharp iron pickets, but as the gate was kept locked, was in fact rusted locked forever, climbing over was the only way to get in, and if she was going, he was too. She took his hand in hers and, his fear confusing his sensibilities, James Blue at that moment felt an urge he could not quite define . . . whether it was to empty his bowels or to take her now, he wasn't sure. He had held off so long. He was going to have this girl but he was determined to have her right, only when she wanted it. (And too, when he could be certain what she would do afterward; they had been regularly warned about underage girls at the base.) But the darkness, the fear, his being out of control excited him and he had it in him then and there to lay her down and get it over with. Lolly pulled him on.

"You haven't met Sexton yet," he thought she said.

James stumbled over roots and small gravestones half-ingested by weeds. Johnson grass and milkweed wrapped about his ankles. Furious at himself for allowing her to put him in a situation she had control over, he had no idea what lay ahead, but when they reached the tree, relaxed a bit: it was at least a landmark, something to hold on to. And then his mind moved on, grew crafty. It was a perfect place, in the crotch of the tree . . . no wonder she had winked . . . a strange place for their first time, he thought; nonetheless, he would take it or any other, especially since she was so enthusiastic, and wore such a wide-hemmed skirt.

She was backed up to the tree and he leaned forward and kissed her, but her response was yet another siege of giggling.

"James," she said, "I want you to meet Sexton."

She drew him around to the other side of the tree.

There was something large there, which he hadn't seen

before because of the tree. It was a huge stone, as tall as the iron gates . . . tall and straight and rounded at the top, no different from the others except in size. As the moon's light was on it, he could tell it was pure marble, swirled and turning, shining like white skin in water. The decapitated angel stood just past it, outside the shelter of the oak. James turned to get back to what had been happening up until the time she led him behind the tree, but Lolly egged him on around to the other side of the stone. Her persistence annoyed him, he didn't want to be distracted or lose the edge they had established, and so it was in irritation that he approached the stone and went round to the other side of it, Lolly close at his heels.

The crickets had hushed the moment they stepped from the car and now there was only the solid weight of silence to fill his ears and run through his head. Once he left the protection of the tree, nothing lay ahead to guide him or let him know what was beyond a footstep. He could not see anything except the endless cotton rows, turned but unplanted. Waiting, lit by a sliver of moon as thin as a fingernail paring, they seemed at the horizon, to curve in toward one another and merge. The crickets, the owl, the rats, the tree frog crouched low in the oak, quietly waited for them to finish and go.

James was looking at his feet, searching for a path, when the presence of something just behind him, just over his head, began to prey on him. Was someone watching? He turned around quickly. Yes. A man. A huge man, lit by the moon, its pale soft light drifting through the tree, illuminating his bowed head. Backing off, James tripped over a small gravestone and fell flat. His tailbone hit something, a root perhaps, and sent shots of pain up his back. He moved backward, using the cheeks of his butt to propel him, as much to relieve the pain as to get farther away from what had startled him. Lolly was laughing like crazy. James Blue lost his erection then and any sexual desire he'd had, but the other urge, the lower one, intensified. He turned to Lolly, terrified, humiliated, outraged, in pain; outraged because of his own fear and humiliated because of the secret looseness in his bowels.

"Don't be afraid, James," she said in mocking assuagement. "Sexton's been dead fifty years."

It was a bronze statue of a knight in armor, his hands clasping the hilt of a sword the tip of which rested between his feet. The statue was large, seven or eight feet, and bulky. His head was draped in chain mail, his hands ensconced in gloves, his feet in socklets of mail. His eyes were down, almost covered by the eyelids, but the way the moonlight hit his protruding eyebrows and cast shadows down his face you could tell they were fierce and strong and full of gloom. His mouth, deep in shadows, was thick—sensuous almost— and it turned down at the corners. His jaw was hard and square. He was overwhelmingly *sad*, though not defeated. Strong . . . as if victory had been the greatest disappointment of all. Behind him, on the stone, was a lengthy inscription.

James got up, rubbing his sore tailbone.

"That's his wife Corrie Ann buried underneath the angel. And this," she pointed to the stone, "is from *Ivanhoe*. It's a poem about death."

Lolly was looking wistfully up at the statue. She thought it was beautiful. To see yourself as a knight, that was reaching the dream you longed for, the silver one. That was getting as high as the moon and shining there forever, where no

one could reach you again or bring you down, like being the
Lolly Ray Lasswell of the *world,* somehow.

"They say he ordered it from New Orleans before he
died, had a special sculptor do it, find the inscription and everything, and had it put in his will that he be buried right
here beneath this oak tree so he'd be cool summers, even
though he wasn't exactly right next to Corrie Ann, there."

His elbows were lifted from his side and his hands were
together on the sword, making a spacious oval in front of
him, waist high. Lolly slipped inside the arms and put her
hands over his, cool and heavy and immortal, while James
flexed his spine and brushed at his clothes. It was mad to be
in a cemetery at the end of a dirt road in the middle of a
cotton field looking up at a statue of Ivanhoe . . . mad.
Lolly, pale silver in the moonlight, bent back her head and
looked up at the knight's face—his head bowed over her as if
in benediction—then turned to James again, her hands still
on the knight's and began to laugh. She was wild with glee.
She looked hard, victorious, nothing like the twirler he knew
on the street, with no smile of promise for him then, not a
hint. It frightened James Blue, who had a wife and child
waiting in Chicago, who was only fooling with Lolly to see
how it would be with a shining gold twirler with tassels on
her boots . . . how many chances would you get for something like that . . . it frightened him almost enough to make
him forget about Lolly and leave her alone . . . almost. But
if she was having her triumph now, he would have his later.
And James Blue was stubborn; once he started something he
finished it.

Still trembling, his heart still crimped in leftover fear, his
knees feeling slightly unhinged, he took her by the hand,
she came out from under the knight's arms and they left. He

thought he heard Granny laughing when they passed her
house. As soon as he got to one, James pulled over to a service station and asked to use the facilities.

The minute they closed the car door, the crickets had
lifted their legs, and resumed their concert with tree frog
and owl. Having seen it all before.

When spring was at its peak, Granny Peavey's house
turned into a veritable paradise of color. There was no grass
at all in her yard, it having been run down once too often by
children and dogs and those broken-down cars Esker was always going to fix up and race at some stock-car track. But
her flowers were a sight. No one in the county had flowers
like Granny Peavey's; of course no one else lived in the most
fertile alluvium-rich land ever put on earth either. In every
imaginable kind of container there were flowers. There were
lard cans of geraniums and bushel baskets running over
with hens and chickens and purple wandering Jew. A cast-
iron pot once used for making soap now overflowed with
portulaca and periwinkle, while an abandoned wringer-type
washing machine erupted honeysuckles down its sides and
over the wringer. A tree stump had been obscured by a
neighboring wisteria vine, which grew from a thick, ropelike
stem and branched out all around, sporting umbrella spokes
of purple grapelike clusters. Baby's breath, mist in an old
hubcap; pansies, velvet in a cracked chamber pot; bleeding
hearts and forget-me-nots in a washtub: the colors were
breathtaking. (Zhena said she ought to get proper flower-
pots from a nursery, that only niggers planted flowers in
hubcaps and washing machines. The pots she brought remained stacked and unused.) Out there in that cotton field,

where what was planted was meant to bring profit or in the case of the graveyard to stay planted and not bloom, sweet-peas grew like precious jewels up a string. Outlining the front porch, giant yellow sunflowers and tissue-thin holly-hocks nodded, the hollyhocks running in hues from white to yellow to a bright red, a deep purple and a gorgeous flamingo salmon. They stood like big sisters protecting the small children at their knees . . . red gladiola, pink phlox, orange marigolds, and all colors of zinnias . . . orange, yel-low, red, and even a pale mint green, a new strain. (Ought to be more particular, Zhena fumed. Ought to pick a few kinds of flowers and stick with them instead of planting just everything that comes along. It's cheap-looking, like a nigger house.) There were strings zigzagged up and down from the roof of the front porch to its floor to guide the morning glories, which made an almost impenetrable barrier to the house and a fine shade for the front porch. Granny sat behind the vines in a rush-seat straight-back rocker Matthew had cut and made himself, crocheting doilies, spit-ting snuff into a baking powder can, swearing, singing, howling. But if a car came—which wasn't often—she got quiet, so that if you went there you couldn't tell from your car whether she was behind the morning glories or not, but most to be on the safe side assumed she was. When Preston Cunningham came to call, he didn't usually get out of his car but often just leaned out the window and yelled, "Mrs. Peavey! You change your mind?" assuming she was there. And from behind the wall of flowers, closed or open depend-ing on the time of day he came by, came in response a loud raucous, "I TOLD YOU *NO*, CUNNINGHAM!" Then he'd drive on, unmoved, thinking one of these days she'd either change her mind or die. Other times he came in and had coffee with her and they passed the time of day together. Granny was pleasant enough to Preston, and he enjoyed her company. They spoke of the weather, the times, the earth and how it chose to yield or not. Granny listened closely to what Preston said, her milky, near-colorless eyes fixed implacably on his. Her body was large and squashed-looking, but her head was so small it seemed shrunken. Her skin was brown and wrinkled; a walnut head, topped with thin wisps of white hair which she twisted in a knot behind her ears. She crocheted, spat, and listened as Preston spoke, as if he were under scrutiny for some crime. She never missed a word of what he said.

Granny walked from container to container during planting time, swearing under her breath, pushing seeds into the earth with one bent finger, which by the end of the sowing was black to the second knuckle. She sowed them in anger and nourished them with rage (but placed them carefully, pushing the larger seeds, such as sunflowers, deep into the earth so that they would be stable and stand tall, and broadcast the tiny flakes that were marigold seeds, gently watering them in: in this as in everything she did, Granny knew exactly what she was about and always profited). And like the dogs and doilies, the flowers thrived and blossomed. She cursed them. "Fucking geraniums," she'd whisper, "goddam sweetpea don't ever want to climb right . . . pissant verbena running over everything . . . piss on you, verbena!" Dared them not to bloom. (But was careful to water them properly.) Cursed the heavens for too much rain when the earth turned to gumbo and too little when it cracked and became dust. Still . . . as if afraid not to . . . they thrived.

She watched Cunningham trucks come and go down the

dirt road, bringing choppers, hoers, planters, and pickers to
the field in a heavy growling old truck with an aluminum
water cooler attached to the back, dripping as it went. One
dog . . . same one every time . . . chased it when it passed;
others didn't bother. She watched them go out early in the
morning during those seasons they were needed, loaded
with people standing looking over the side of the truck,
leaning on whatever tool was needed for whatever job had
to be done that time of year. Then about three o'clock, the
trucks would whine back past, still dripping water, the people still standing leaning on their tools looking exactly as
they had going out, even after a whole day's work looking
no hotter or tireder or more resigned than they had that
morning. It was only by the direction the truck was going in
that she could tell if they were headed out or coming back
in again, because nothing in their faces yielded as much as a
clue. If it was picking time, another truck came to load up
the big burlap sacks they had pulled all day like cockroaches
dragging egg sacs and filled with the day's harvest; otherwise, it always looked the same, the expression on the people's faces, the truck, the water, the smells; only the weather
shifted then came back again . . . all year in and year out
converging, blending like colors of paint stirred together.

V

CARROLL

Sitting outside after dinner, Frank often heard echoes of a race . . . cars whining past on 84, headed north toward the next town, engines pushed near to spinning out . . . about which he always made a point of voicing disapproval, not so much of the boys who drove so fast but of parents who provided young people with cars at such an early age then simply turned them loose. It was a well-known race . . . at ten miles, the longest unofficiated one anywhere in the area.

The starting point was just inside the Eunola city limits at the intersection of Highways 84 and 1, where the Gold 'n' Crust Bread Co. was. The time, late; when traffic was sparse and only the all-night cafés were open. (And the Gold 'n' Crust, which baked its bread at night.) At a pre-established time, when the traffic light at that intersection turned green, two cars went screaming north up 84 all the way to the first stoplight in Sunflower, a clear ten miles away, straight north without a curve or hitch, each driver pushing his machine

either to stay ahead of the other one the entire ten miles or
to be close, keeping enough power in reserve to rush ahead
at the end and take it, one way or another to win. They
hoped to establish their place in that way, hoped by calling
a bluff on innocence and fear to earn once and for all the
indifference, the air of authority, the look of knowing their
sex required. It was a way to do it, and it was possible to
gain your self-assurance that way, and once a boy had, he
never lost it entirely; if he never did another thing the rest
of his life he had at least endured this ritual and could
thereby claim rights to his manhood, or, as they called it, his
balls. And while that claim wouldn't carry him, it did help
see him through in his own mind at least. It was also possible if not to say likely to lose his life while purchasing this
dear commodity, but nobody ever said so because it was
also part of the ritual not to speak of the risk, as if what was
gambled was that trivial. Like a rat spying a hunk of cheese
on a set trap, a boy had to keep his mind on one thing and
one only, the cheese. He had to sprint through the trap,
avoid the bar, and pull his tail out before the bar fell, and
most of all, had to hold on to the cheese; dear God, you had
to hold tight to the cheese once you had it and grip it might-
ily with your teeth, because if you didn't get out with the
cheese you might as well never have taken the risk and gone
through. They knew the trap was stretched out ten miles in
front of them, filled with trucks and wet spots and sudden
mechanical failures, and knew what it could do to them if
they weren't fast or clever enough, but they also understood
that if you let your mind stray and thought about *that*, you
not only would never reach the cheese, you'd never even
make it through the traffic light but would be left high and
dry at the Gold 'n' Crust Bread Co., smelling fresh bread,

with everybody saying you didn't yet have what you most wanted to lay claim to, your balls.

Preston Cunningham knew nothing of these ceremonies, but when he drove through town in the new car he had bought Carroll, he did find out by what people said and how they acted that they already knew he was getting it, had been waiting since he ordered it to see it, and were not at all surprised what make or model car it was, yet because of the way it looked could not resist stopping to admire it and gawk at it and nudge others to do the same: it was that grand. Boys gathered together after seeing it, wondering, *was this the one?* Could it be and if it was, would they know? Would Carroll put it on the line? Who knew? Nobody was friendly with Carroll, so who could say? They trembled with wanting to know these things but had to hold out until he got home to find out. And even then there was the possibility he would not stay in Eunola but would take his gift and go off somewhere, to Memphis or some camp or other . . . and even if he did stay, if his personality was anything like his father's, it wasn't likely the boy would be too sporting.

Keeping the new car at home for a surprise, Preston drove his own Oldsmobile to pick Carroll up and right away . . . once they were settled and headed back toward Eunola . . . asked his son about going to college in the fall. But Carroll refused: he had had enough school. It had taken him an extra year to get out of the academy they had sent him to as it was, and he had no intention of voluntarily heading right back to some other institution, not right away. And Preston said that was all right, he could stay home for a while and work on the place, at the gin or in the office, maybe even until the first of the year. But then Carroll would have to make up his mind to do one thing or another or the draft would get him. (Not having had much practical experience as a father, Preston thought that when a father said you can do this thing but not this other that it automatically meant something to a son and that Carroll would automatically pay some attention to what he was saying, being a son listening to his father give advice.) But the boy did not respond. He had been taught early to reserve his fears and deepest feelings and by now he was as cut off from them as if his heart were wrapped in a web. He sat coolly on the other side of the car, looking out the window as if what was outside interested him, keeping an easy distance from the man driving. They were strangers, each in his own private world; only one thing came between them to tie them in any way to one another, and that was the person at home making up her face to prepare herself for her son's appearance: Lady. The one point they kept coming back to, in all their uncertain wanderings, the stationary center around which the two of them revolved. Lady. Who could not hold her hand still to put her mouth on correctly and finally gave up and smeared some color on with a finger tip.

These were the first words of advice Preston had spoken to his son. He only said them now because he thought it was time to; since Carroll was practically a man, and needed some information with which to face the world. And that was all; just that he thought it must be time. But Preston had nothing to say to Carroll that Carroll cared to hear, much less pay heed to. He was going back to Eunola all right, not to work at the gin or prepare for college, but to do the things he'd not been free to, to get out of that uniform and into decent clothes, to see what it was like to live in a town and drive around free and easy like other boys. And when they got home and Preston showed him the car, Carroll only said, "Thanks, Dad," with no gratitude, then went inside and spoke briefly to Lady, his heart pounding. She lay back in her chaise longue, waving him near. But when he bent to greet her, she turned her head and lifted one hand slightly to keep him from getting too close, and so Carroll quickly withdrew . . . said goodbye, got in his new car, and left. And as he drove toward town, he looked from the outside as cool and calm, as totally enveloped in self and solitude as he always had. The origin of his gray-green gaze seemed just as far removed from this world and time as ever, his feelings just as much inside his skull beating against bone to get out. Nobody would have guessed how he felt. The muscles in his jaw shifted and ground as he took the car out the gravel and down the blacktop road to town. It was a hot May night . . . Eunola schools were still in session . . . and the air was filled with mosquitoes and a damp river-heavy oppressiveness. But though the new car had factory-installed air conditioning, Carroll did not use it but opened up the windows and stuck his elbow out and breathed in the terrible hot air.

He was tall and thin and walked with an easy gait, his head slightly cocked to one side. His hair was blond, close-cropped, his face long and angular. He swaggered. No one ever felt at ease with Carroll; he never seemed to join anything but instead was always the one providing materials for other people's enjoyment . . . which after a while, they came to resent. If Carroll had known as he drove his new car downtown how scared the boys at the local drive-in restaurant were of *him*, of his calm grace and green-eyed haughtiness and indifference, he might have faced them with less trepidation, but military school had given him little preparation for such confrontations and so as he pulled in the one vacant parking place and watched the crowd gathered at the other end saunter over, he was, beneath the nonchalance the others assumed was his truest attitude, terrified.

It took the car to break the ice. Because that was all that counted. Important things happened in cars. Momentous things. And if you had the right car, you were simply the right person, and that was it.

Carroll's to begin with was a Buick, which was quite a beginning. Not that Buick was necessarily *the* car for a boy to have that year because it wasn't; most of them preferred older, lighter cars and that summer a five-year-old Mercury was most in favor, and if they'd had a choice most of them would not have chosen a Buick, so it wasn't that . . . but Buick was not just a car, and not just a big car, and not just a big expensive car but simply the car of all cars: the one. Buick meant flash, class, and size right away, right now without looking; if you had a Buick, you had that going for you, that response, that quick upward roll of the eyeballs, that gift of easy light. There were people who argued for other big cars—Oldsmobiles and Chryslers, even Pontiacs (Cadillac advocates were in a class to themselves, and didn't talk cars at all but simply ordered a new Caddy fall after fall)—but when it came down to the nut of it, those others were arguing only in opposition to, in resistance to *the* car, the one, Buick, because Buick was by and large by prevailing standards, *IT*. So when an eighteen-year-old boy was given a brand-new Buick all his own just for getting out of high school and then doing it a year late, well, that was an event worth noting at least. (Preston's reasons for buying weren't clear even to himself. But Preston believed in the efficacy of things; if it was time for a thing to be done it should be, whatever the cost. Needful of duties, he thought it was proper that Carroll have a new car, and since they were well enough off, he might as well have a good one.)

But Buick wasn't even all.

That was only the beginning.

Carroll didn't just get any Buick. Preston didn't just go down and order any brand-new Buick for his only son but went and ordered the biggest, heaviest Buick made.

"You hear what Carroll Cunningham's getting for graduation?"

"Yeah. I heard."

"What?"

"Buick."

"Naw."

"Yeah . . . a Buick."

"Naw. You ain't heard. You ain't heard nothing. Only maybe half of it, hearing Buick. But not just. Carroll Cunningham's getting a *Roadmaster*."

Roadmaster. The one. As heavy and big as they came: Roadmaster.

As heavy in appearance as a two-ton truck, the Roadmaster was not sleek or racy and not feisty but solid, like a hunk of pure lead. It had four doors and a trunk as big as a cave and foot space enough for seven six-footers; it had chrome up and down the trunk, chrome back and forth along the sides, chrome on top of the hood, chrome sparkling in the grille, and chrome all over the dash. The steering wheel was flat and thick, laced with chrome, and the upholstery felt as soft as bunny fur. All Buicks had chrome-encircled exhaust holes along the front fenders, holes which didn't serve as any kind of exhaust but were

merely decorative and identifying. Exhaust holes meant
Buick. Now the small Special Buick had three exhaust holes
and so did the slightly larger Super, but the biggest and the
most Buick had four, which marked it, branded it Roadmaster, as well as two extra chrome strips over its backside
plus the natural fact that nobody ever mistook it for anything else if they had any idea at all what was what in the
first place. The grille looked like a mouth . . . wide open
with its top lip curled back and its teeth bared, grinning like
some Richard Widmark movie character threatening no telling what harm. And to top it off and make the air of menace
complete, it had—left and right at just about where the
mouth's incisors would be—two inserts of useless decorative
chrome, smooth and round and pointed at the end, shaped
like nothing so much as bullets. So it seemed the mouth was
armed. Ready to fire.

"Can't you just see it!" one carless boy exclaimed, hoping
for the best from the Roadmaster. "Can't you just see Fillian's face when he gets a look at those *bullets!*"

Over the grille, atop the hood where Pontiac put an In-
dian head and Chevy a pair of wings was a solid heavy
ring of chrome big enough to fit a man's forearm (and often
did; those rings were a prize across town, where they
adorned many a black man's arm, as measure of *his* prestige
and legend). Carroll's Roadmaster was two-toned green,
dark green on top and a mint color below, striped in between with all that chrome and interrupted along the side
with those four silver-circled exhaust holes serving no mechanical function. It had air conditioning, automatic push-
button windows, fifteen-inch tires, and a band of swirled
spun aluminum across the dash; a radio and an armrest for
the driver. Its windshields were tinted dark bluish-green

and its speedometer went horizontally across the dash, starting near the window on the driver's side, going halfway across to the other, its indicator a slim red streak that moved from left to right and number to number ending in a 45-degree-angled point which told you how fast you were going. When the car stopped, the red streak went down inside the dash as if swallowed up. The Roadmaster squatted. Hunkered low. Solid. Inside, the engine hummed so low you almost couldn't hear it . . . rumbling steady and sweet as night itself, it was Buick's own exclusive transmission, Dynaflow. Which rounded the whole thing out and gave it the name that made it what it was, a Roadmaster with Dynaflow.

"Still . . ." doubtful boys said, "*still.*"

It was a man's car and most of them were dubious, thinking of Jimmy Fillian, a duck-tailed high school dropout with sorry teeth and a cockeye, who had come all the way across the bridge from Pigeon Hole, Arkansas, back in January to take the ten-miler in his customized six-year-old Ford, then had returned in March and again in April to keep the title. The race had become that well known, that people came from all over to participate, and when Carroll got his Roadmaster, Eunola was sorely in need of a serious contender of its own. And so when he came in town that night they asked him right away, and though he knew nothing of the race, Carroll said yes, sure, let's give it a try, and they went out Highway 84 to the intersection and put the Roadmaster on the line.

And then . . . a week later . . . gave it the real test.

Jimmy Fillian came cruising into town. Popping his steel packs, combing his glistening forelock into a slow hanging curl, Jimmy, like most drivers, traveled alone, unwilling to take the risk of being slowed by extra weight. And when he rolled into the drive-in parking lot in his high whining Ford and took one look at what was supposed to be his big competition, that big heavy squatting Roadmaster straight out of a showroom, that solid and spacious family kind of car with all its chrome and useless weight, and then at Carroll, so skinny and military school naïve, so easygoing and clean, then back over at his Ford with its stolen fender skirts and dual exhausts, hunkered down heavy in the back with lowering blocks, and thought about the beautiful three-two carburetors shining like moons under the hood and the Mallory dual point ignition he'd worked overtime to buy and the high compression heads and the loud rattling smitties, which police on both sides of the river and in between had warned him had to go . . . and then looked back one more time at Carroll with his hair cut short, wearing plain white button-down Oxford cloth and ironed and creased khaki pants and clean white tennis shoes, and when he saw all the kids Carroll was letting ride with him . . . on the *race* . . . Jimmy Fillian never hesitated saying why not, slicking back his duck-tails one more time, pulling his cockeye in as near a straight line as he could, thinking this time he had himself a sucker.

The two drove slowly out 84 to the bakery. There, from the full entourage trailing them, a boy from another car got out and lined the cars up exactly even. Jimmy's kept roaring forward too soon, jumping the gun. Meant for getting up and going, not for waiting around, the car was hard to contain; it wanted to *move on*. But finally the boy said okay they were even, and when another red light came on he moved out of the way. When it changed to green, they'd be off.

The aroma of Gold 'n' Crust Bread wafted over them and hung softly in the hot night air, but they didn't smell it, neither the ones in the two cars racing nor any of the others parading behind, all of them too filled with their own smells, of boot oil and hair oil and young nervousness to smell anything else.

Jimmy Fillian started gunning his motor while the light was still red, racing it, his foot three quarters of the way down, while Carroll sat as patiently as an old man waiting downtown for a light to change. Six other kids hung out the Buick's windows, screaming and yelling and beating their hands against the sides of the car. Jimmy never looked over or heard; he had his good eye trained steadily on the stoplight and one foot tensed down holding the accelerator exactly so . . . ready . . . and the other on the clutch, keeping the engine high and set to go. The instant the red light went off, Jimmy popped his clutch and took off screaming, up to forty in first, to sixty-five in third, to ninety–ninety-five–one hundred and ten in twenty seconds flat, speed shifting all the way, his motor whining high, his head loosening up with the speed unleashed, flying free. He had left Carroll sitting at the intersection like a stop sign. No one else had left either. In fact, Jimmy Fillian wasn't even sure Carroll's car had come away at all or if maybe he was still back at Highway 1 at the bread company because the Roadmaster wasn't to be seen . . . not anywhere close. Was it a joke? Jimmy, when he passed the Dairy Delite, checking and rechecking his rearview mirror, eased off a bit, and came back down to ninety-five, which if he could hold it would more than likely be fast enough. Frowning, he looked from the road to the mirror, thinking what he'd do to Carroll if it had been a joke, how he'd take him apart, how . . . but then he saw, back, way far back, a car. With wide-apart headlights. It could be a Buick. And, continuing to look and check while keeping his eye on the road ahead and his mind on his own business, Jimmy finally decided that, yes, it was a Buick, it had to be Carroll because there were other lights behind him, and he thought he even saw the gleam of teeth grinning in the light of those hard round eyes, and silver bullets between the incisors of those teeth. It was the Roadmaster all right, coming, moving but not fast, not gaining, or if it was, awful damn slow. "Shit!" Jimmy exclaimed out loud. "*Shit!*" The rich boy was as slow as he looked. And all this time the Ford was screaming, whining, doing ninety-five and a hundred, straining and pushing to make the whole ten miles at top speed without letup. Jimmy passed a car; a truck; another car. But he was fidgety. With Carroll poking along not even past the Dairy Delite yet, it wasn't like a contest at all, and he found it hard to keep an edge on: Jimmy needed opposition, something to go against, to keep his back up and his reflexes sharp. This was nothing. He lit a Chesterfield, and holding it between his teeth, squinting at the smoke drifting up to his eyes, figured when he got a few miles farther it would be safe to slow down some . . . no sense pushing any harder than he had to . . . if Carroll was still so far back. All the time checking again and again in the mirror for the Roadmaster, which he could still see, as well as the lights behind, but could not *feel*, the way he liked to, it was too far back.

Halfway between Eunola and Sunflower, just past the trailer park, Jimmy thought it was time to ease off, but when he checked the mirror he was surprised to find the headlights behind him were just a little bigger, not much but . . . yes, sure enough, they were; the Buick was pulling up a

little, nothing threatening, just a casual kind of closing of
the gap. Which gave Jimmy a welcome bit of rev and hard-
ened his nerve some. He swelled up just thinking of that
fat-assed car with its rich skinny driver getting close. Closing slow and too late . . . since he was past halfway now
and all but impossible to beat with the lead he had. And so
he didn't worry but dragged hard on his Chesterfield and
said out loud "Easy, Greasy . . . you got a long way to
slide." And laughed again, thinking of the story he'd tell
back in Pigeon Hole, already making it up in his mind as if
he were saying it, then hearing himself laugh and tell his
friends how when he got back from the race the Roadmaster
was still at the stoplight and he guessed they had stopped
off to buy themselves a loaf of *bread!* Jimmy rubbed his
palm across the rolled and tucked custom-fitted black and
white naugahyde interior of his car . . . God, how he loved
that car. How many hours he had spent with his duck-tailed
head deep in its engine. How meticulously he cared for it,
kept it, lubed and waxed and cleaned it. How lovingly he
maintained its every part. He checked the mirror again.
Bigger still. The bared teeth were plainer now, and he could
see arms hanging out the windows beating against the side
of the car. The parade was farther back now, as the Roadmaster pulled away. Jimmy felt an itch between his thighs, a
low-grade tingle, some heat. Lifting his butt slightly, shifting his weight, he reset himself for the contest, put out his
cigarette, and began to feel it now . . . actually to *feel* the
moving-up of the car. A prickling cold climbed his scalp, a
slow sure inching, and then Jimmy saw the bullets clearly.
The chrome grille sparkled in the lights and the teeth were
getting closer and the Roadmaster kept coming and kept
coming, and Jimmy was already going as fast as he could,

his right foot flat on the floor. And still the Roadmaster kept coming and coming, doing an honest one hundred fifteen miles an hour, a speed which did not strain or push its low rumbling humming engine in the least and never had. That patented Dynaflow had never shifted, which was how it worked, not by shifting but by slowly, cylinder by cylinder, *catching*. Gathering speed with each catch, slowly—dumb— like a snowball rolling down a gradual slope picking up more and more snow, patiently working its way down, gathering weight and momentum so that you hardly notice it's getting bigger until at the bottom of the gentle incline you look up and a small avalanche is on you. The Roadmaster had started off at Highway 1 rumbling low, had passed the Dairy Delite rumbling low, and was still, at a hundred fifteen miles an hour, rumbling low. The only difference was it was going fast now. Carroll had pushed the accelerator all the way to the floor when the light turned green, and the Roadmaster had responded by barely moving at all, as sluggish as cold syrup. It had just *eased* across the intersection, as it always did, no faster and no slower than if he'd only tapped the accelerator in no hurry. Then, as the outside cylinders of the Dynaflow one by one caught on, the car had slowly started very steadily gaining; with no fanfare or outward indication of strain, only very steadily like that snowball had begun picking up speed, picking it up and picking it up. And the red arrow of the speedometer had moved just as slowly and as inexorably across the dash, a mile at a time; one mile, another, another . . . the engine all the time as low and sluggish and heavy as ever, never showing the least sign of life or pep or vitality, just steadily and slowly changing from a slow-moving car into a fast-moving one. And very steadily Carroll moved up on Jimmy Fillian, who could have

beat the Roadmaster a thousand times over in a scratch-off
contest or even a five-mile race but not this one, this was another thing entirely; it took a will for distance and a capacity
for high speed over the long run. It was hard for any car to
run an honest one-fifteen for any distance at all much less
ten clear miles, and Jimmy's couldn't, but Carroll's seemed
likely to. Jimmy felt trapped; he slammed his right foot
down as if to push the accelerator through the floor, and still
the Ford stayed at its usually adequate one hundred and the
Roadmaster kept crawling up and the Ford was, under
Jimmy's urgent pressure, beginning to sound as if it might
spin out any minute, and Carroll coming yet. He sat straight
and steady as a rock in the Roadmaster, his foot pushed to
the floor, the engine humming low and easy, but not pressing, just cruising out at a steady honest unwavering one-
fifteen. With four hundred pounds of extra weight hanging
out the windows. Carroll had his left elbow out the window
and just two fingers of his left hand on the wheel. His right
arm was on the armrest that separated him from his compan-
ions, and the radio was on and he was swinging his right
hand to the beat of the music, as if he were out for a Sunday's casual drive, cruising down Main Street at dusk. Jimmy
Fillian muttered and cursed while Carroll sat quiet and
calm, the nonchalance of his heritage giving him an edge
. . . just moving on, until about two miles from Sunflower
he was side by side with Jimmy Fillian, as he had from the
first known he eventually would be. The others jeered and
shouted and cursed and fell back holding their sides laughing. Carroll finally looked over from his straight-ahead
stance. Just once. He turned in Jimmy's direction, tipped an
imaginary hat and kind of half-assed smiled. And Jimmy
Fillian in his duck-tails and yellow teeth, with his cockeye

streaming, saw him and pushed his Ford until it boiled.
Jimmy's heart surged and throbbed as the Roadmaster
moved on by, steady and sure, to Sunflower, where Carroll
treated his riders and followers to beer and pizza, while the
Roadmaster sat quiet and calm in the parking lot, altogether
unbothered by the race, not in any way overheated. But the
Ford rattled by, coughing and limping, then turned around
and to the young Eunolites' cheers headed back to Arkansas
and sputtered across the bridge, smoking, begging its feverish owner for a rest.

Carroll sipped his beer and listened to the others laugh
and howl at his victory. Although he had participated in the
race and had won and had enjoyed it well enough, he felt no
part of it. It didn't touch him.

At school, when Carroll had thought of home, he chiefly
remembered Lady. How she drifted, her blond hair in that
perfect pageboy, a soft tube lying across her slim white
shoulders like grace itself. And how she never was bothered
or seemed touched . . . never responding, moving alone
from room to room, light as a cloud, and yet in some way
not light and soft at all, but hard, remote. "Dear," she had
whispered to him years back, so far he could not recall
when. "Please . . . call me *Lady*." That voice was like steel.
He would never forget it; she meant for him not to. Lady.
She had long red fingernails and matching lips . . . a
reddish-purple, like a color in dreams. She kept her body
slim and lithe by exercising every morning . . . which, home
for holidays he could hear: in his room, he woke to the
sound of her bump-bumping on the floor and wall next to
him, hitting her hips against it, walking feet up it as she lay

on the floor. She let him come so close and no farther. Any time he threatened her with the least suggestion of dependence or need, she punished him with her indifference.

She took pride in wearing no bra or girdle . . . it was a scandal in town . . . even when golfing. And summers, under her careful scheduling, turned her body to a deep golden bronze, her legs, shaved to the groin, set off by wide-legged white shorts. Her face was perfect, immovable. She was contained, a unity within herself, drifting, disconnected from everything and everyone, except perhaps Serenthea, who trailed along protecting her. She was slick and golden. That was how he remembered her. That was how she had been for years. So beautiful and sure, meticulously preserving herself. Until more recent visits, when he couldn't recall her wearing shorts any more . . . or clothes of any kind except loose silky things, lounging clothes, pajamas and robes and gowns. No more ribbons tied in her hair while gardening (which meant going out and telling Judge where to plant and what to dig up). No more soft skirts at dinner. Only the drifting . . . room to room.

As for Preston . . .

He hardly thought of him at all. Stout, bald, fever-faced and flustered, a man too easily read, who worked in the field like a hand and at home orbited around Lady like a forgotten star going bright to dim, turning tricks, winking, plummeting . . . anything; begging attention.

As Carroll did. Each time he went home, despite his intentions, he found himself anxious to see her, his heart so full of hope and expectation it weighed him down. Looking for a reprieve, a glance, the click of unmitigated love, unqualified acceptance. In the light of her indifference, the old threads around his heart wrapped tighter, exiling hope. And he received nothing, not even a crumb. In this, he was no less obvious than Preston.

The race was meaningless. Who he wanted to impress seemed beyond his reach.

But now he had a chance, now that things were different. After all, he was home for good now, living there at last. He followed Lady about, watching as she closed herself up in her room to be waited on by Serenthea, who so carefully locked her door as she went out. Examining the pattern of her days, he awaited an explanation. Something to tell him why there was such a gap between what she had made him believe and what he himself actually saw. He would get to her yet. There was plenty of time now.

VI

TOWN
CHARACTERS

There were special people in Eunola whose lives and the treatment they received gave good testimony to how the town operated and was constituted on a day-to-day routine level . . . what people liked and disliked, who and what they were prejudiced against, which manners it was important to know. That these special people were granted dispensation from those traditions and ordinary customs said more about those in a position to make the grants than those who were the beneficiaries.

But the testimony was neither plainspoken nor loud. You had to listen very carefully to the ones who knew, and to find out which clues were the key ones you had to have inside information as to who was who and what was what because the laws and by-laws were spoken either in whispers behind cupped hands or, often, not at all, in the case of those assumptions which were silently understood among them with no need for reiteration.

Take, for instance, the case of Tillman Hughes. Tillman, a lawyer, had lived in Eunola for eight years and had plainly decided to stay. An ambitious person, Tillman for those eight years had been searching for the right platform from which to speak a speech he had written, one which would advertise his rightness and raise his standing in the town and give him the respectability, possibly even if he was lucky the *prestige* both he and his law practice so far lacked. But though he thought he had found it, an unshakable base whose integrity he felt no one could question, Tillman understood neither the ongoing structure of standards in Eunola nor the terms under which special dispensation from those standards was awarded, nor the necessity of knowing certain rules of etiquette . . . he did not know, in short, how to behave. He *almost* did, though, and because it egged him on and made him hope and think he did, that *almost* caused Tillman Hughes's ruin, not just in Eunola but inside himself as well . . . in a way *not* knowing never would have. (In some cases, it seems, and in this Eunola was no different from a thousand thousand other towns in a thousand thousand other times, having half a loaf is far more dangerous than having no bread at all.)

To those with an ear for nuance, it would never turn out: "interdenominational" sounded queer and "interfaith" was even worse, having a distinctly *Jewish* ring to it. And what was wrong with church, anyway? But Tillman Hughes stood up and assured people that this organization called Young People for Christ was on the up-and-up, an association dedicated to the reclamation of teen-aged souls, a worthy goal, no one could doubt. And because Tillman was honest enough, if a newcomer, and because so many youngsters begged to go, many Eunolites one summer took his word and sent their offspring to an YPC-sponsored interdenominational camp in the clouds, where they were supposed to find . . . among crags and creeks and Western sunsets, amidst fields of Rocky Mountain wildflowers and other wonders of Nature . . . Jesus.

And many of them did.

They came home with memorized Bible verses like pop songs in their heads and the light of revealed truth shining from their eyes, which were fixed within, focused on the hero who fired their imaginations: St. Paul, the blond and loving muscleman, burly and gentle, castigating and loving, tough but forgiving, like a Big Eight fullback gone to preaching in tents. And if Paul was their darling, John 3:16 was the watchword. If after all for love of this wayward world God had sacrificed his only . . . only! . . . begotten son then who could distrust that love, who not want everlasting life, who not desire never to perish, who, and in his name and for his sake forever, amen . . . who?

Now although it was situated well within the boundaries, Eunola was not one of your true Bible Belt towns at all, much to the regret and delicious horror of the exiled teetotaling Baptists, those gaunt ladies who waited not for Lolly on Friday afternoon parades, but the band, and dared not look at her except to reconfirm their suspicions. And most people there—at least the ones in position to send their children to a rather expensive camp in the first place and therefore the only ones Tillman cared about speaking to about YPC—did not take their religion overly seriously. That is, they didn't get fanatical about it, not like the nut Christians on the outskirts of town, those Holy Rollers who wouldn't go

to dances or wear lipstick or watch television, who parked
cars without engine hoods in front yards. And not like Cath-
olics and serious Baptists who changed their lives to fit their
religion, no: the majority of Eunolites didn't bow too low or
pray overlong but worshiped only to the absolute minimum
weekly requirements of ritual, self-denial and fervor, and
felt that they had in that way done their duty by church. Go
Sundays, keep the Golden Rule; that was enough. Starting
at the top with Episcopalians, those lapsed aristocrats,
church was more a means of social categorization than any
kind of worshiping ceremony. So a lot of parents, Christian
parents at that, weren't as thrilled as you might think when
their offspring came home from the mountains describing
evening campfires before which they and other young
campers confessed past sins and dedicated their lives to
Jesus and then and there became . . . praise the Lord . . .
saved.

Saved? Decorous and staid Presbyterians, who didn't
kneel to pray or take to the altar for Communion but sat
where they were, stiff in straightback pews, waiting for the
Light to come to them, who were nothing if not indignant in
the face of sin . . . *saved?*

It was a Baptist word. They weren't comfortable.

And when the children went on, describing the love circle
and the morning meditations held on a rock in the middle of
a creek bed, where they were totally silent and communed
with nature, allowing the wonder of God to enter them, and
when they swooned over cool, strong St. Paul, and recited
their verses . . . in order, as arranged in small packets of
cards, each carrying one verse . . . as if they were still
young enough to bone up on the catechism which they'd all
been through as children . . . and sighed about the recep-

tion of a new lamb into the flock, well, by then, "interdenominational" was beginning to sound even more suspect.
Young People for Christ was becoming in their minds more
than a little extreme in the way of religion to these middling
Christians to whom MYP and an occasional Communion
and possibly giving up something for Lent, potatoes or
chewing gum or cigarettes, was, by God, enough. It was certainly skirting the edge of nut Christian.

Still.

Juvenile delinquency, which had been on the rampage,
enjoyed a hiatus that summer as many sons, including Tillman's, sheathed their switchblades for Jesus. And the
weekly meetings of YPC . . . rowdy, joyous affairs, which,
led by an official YPC co-ordinator, rocked to Jesus-saves-
you-and-me songs as well as dedications and rededications
and the voices of young people reciting memorized Bible
verses, in order . . . continued and were held in some of the
best homes of Eunola.

Now one or two individuals investigated YPC in the
hopes of turning up serious flaws but came up with nothing
but hints of, at the very least, nagging and rigorous noncon-
formity. It did originate several states to the north, too, and
while that wasn't of itself necessarily bad, it was never all
good either, things being the way they were. And then, it
was founded by a renegade Methodist preacher who had
divorced his wife and put away his robes and taken another
younger wife and gone on to become fat and wealthy off the
souls of the young. In Jesus' name, amen.

Still. All that was understandable. And who could argue
with Christianity in the young, being themselves Christian?

Most did not. Nothing so far was bad enough to provoke
much more than gripes and frowns.

And so Tillman Hughes congratulated himself. He had got what he needed from the introduction of YPC into Eunola, a modicum of respectability in the eyes of those who counted. He began being needed. He was invited to become a member of a men's civic club; his law business picked up; he spoke before banquets and luncheons on "The Christian Family Today," and for the first time in his life could see visions of prestigiousness rising in his future. Like engraved tablets. Or perhaps, tombstones.

That fall, YPC sent out a three-color brochure announcing a Christmas retreat. It was to be a re-rededication—or rededication or dedication depending on the young soul's condition—to Christ. There were, naturally enough, pictures in the brochure showing young people at the camp romping and playing and singing with fervor and zest. They looked as happy as any youngsters at camp. The camp looked as attractive and as filled with the wonders of nature as any camp, the leaders as healthy and outgoing as any camp counselors, not much different from other camp brochures. On the back cover was a picture of a volleyball game in progress, taken about at the net so that profiles of members of each team were included in the picture. The cover was tinted a bluish color and the picture was so fuzzy that parents looking for their own children and children looking for themselves had a hard time recognizing one from another and telling who was who and so they rummaged around and found magnifying glasses and took closer looks. Still, one child blurred into another . . . except for one . . . there was one who stood out clear enough, one they scrutinized and magnified and finally recognized. Finally, they had found something bad enough to complain about. They called one another up, the parents that is, and those who hadn't got out

their magnifying glasses did, and when they had looked and
made sure, called up other parents to see if they had. And
when all of them had and were convinced, they gathered together and marched to Tillman Hughes's office and con-
fronted him, brochures clenched in their fists.

If the boy had leaned back another quarter to half inch,
he would not have been in the picture at all. As it was, a sta-
ple slashed his eyelid and cheek and ripped through the
corner of his mouth, and all that was left of him was a slice
. . . a tuft of hair, a paring of profile, and above him his arm
stretched high as he leaped to spike the ball across the net,
fingers pointed heavenward. A sliver of boy, thin as an ear-
lobe, as blurred in blue as if enveloped in low-hanging
Rocky Mountain clouds.

"Look!" the parents screamed, "and try to tell us he's *not!*
Look at that nose and that face and the palm of that hand,
Tillman Hughes, and tell us what that boy's doing at a camp
we sent our *children* to."

Our children! Our hope! With that boy.

And Tillman looked, although he already knew, and said,
(rather casually, still not catching on, still deluded and
dragged on by that undying hopeful *almost*), "Well, he's the
cook's son, you see, and as the cook lives on the grounds, the
boy plays an occasional game of volleyball with the kids.
None of them actually *goes* there, of course . . . and this
. . . and this boy . . . and . . ."

Suddenly Tillman saw them anew. Apart from *almost*. A
shield of outraged Christians, grim and unflinching, stood
before his desk, confirmed in their united prejudice, convinced of its rightness, waiting for Tillman to bury himself
up to his neck by defending any organization which allowed any person of another color to join in no telling

what activities with their children, which he did; and they were only too happy to take care of his head. Finally YPC was bad enough. Finally it violated the tender center of their open-mindedness. They were, after all, flexible, free-thinking modern Christians but up to a point, a firm and very stable point.

By noon, it was claimed YPC had been investigated and found to be a communist-front organization (another common threat to their well-being in those days), registered with the FBI and its local co-ordinator, a *card-carrying agent*. All the lingo was dragged out. Even the saved children whispered it. Then . . . with one thing folding in on another so rapidly that pretty soon no one remembered which thing happened in what sequence or if there was any rational logical progress to any of it, Tillman Hughes came under suspicion and soon after that became a person to avoid.

The police never did discover who blew up his mailbox or smashed his office window. Or who set a small fire on his front porch one night. It wasn't until after Tillman finished stomping it out and came back in his house that he realized what had been inside the burning sack and why he had heard laughter as he snuffed its flames, and jeers as he turned to re-enter his house. His wife had run in and screamed, pointing down. There besmirching the pure wool champagne-colored carpeting, curling up around the toes of his high shining wing-tipped shoes, fouling his very life and dreams and hopes, was dung. It's from a *person*, his wife wailed as Tillman sprayed on carpet shampoo. An *adult person!*

That was how they felt about him now . . . and yet it was not so bad, comparatively speaking; there were no burning crosses, no awful threats of bombs, nothing like that, not in Eunola.

Tillman's law practice fell off to nothing, and he spent many hours staring out his window at the sidewalk below, so many as a matter of fact that his foot made a permanent dent in the gas heater next to his desk, where he propped it, sitting idly, passing days.

A lot of people would have packed up and left then and there. But Tillman had only just finished building a split-level house and buying membership in the country club and tithing for that year, and he had paid the first three installments on choice cemetery plots in the Eunola graveyard, in the good part where trees were. Plus, he couldn't see just up and dragging his children away from their friends and school and his wife away from her garden club, now that the trees and flowers and shrubs in their yard were getting of a size and age to bloom. . . . No, he said to himself, it was not the thing to do. (Unspoken, barely dared dreamed, was his hope that as time went on and the incident faded, people would forgive and forget and then give him back his respectability and invite him once again into good standing. Since Eunola was the only town he had ever in his life come so close to being a real part of, he could not bring himself to abandon either the town or the hope.) So he sat. His brother from St. Louis, from whom he had heard about YPC in the first place, called regularly, saying he couldn't get over it, YPC had certainly worked for him. He loaned Tillman a few dollars to tide him over until he got back on his feet again.

While sitting one month with his foot on the heater . . . and then another month . . . Tillman figured out how he could manage to stay in town and still pay his bills. One day it came to him and the next day he got up out of his chair and went out to implement his plan, as quick as that.

On his way out he told his secretary, who sat with a manicure set on her desk, emery boarding her thumbnail while listening to her portable radio, that he would be out all day and that she should take all calls. Shrugging . . . what calls? . . . she nodded and returned her attention to a pesky hangnail. And Tillman was, indeed, out of the office not only that day but the next as well and the next; he was in fact out every day for a week, and by the next, calls did start coming in, and his secretary's nails began going to pot.

Finally, after two full weeks, Tillman returned.

"Who," his employee wanted to know, "are all these *people?*" Not wanting to spell out exactly what she meant by *people,* in that tone of voice, with those pursed lips.

Tillman only smiled.

"Just tell them how to get to the office," he instructed her. "Tell them I will not talk over the phone and they have to come here. Talk slow and keep it simple."

They were poor, the people who started streaming into Tillman Hughes's office in an unending flow, but there were so many of them to begin with and so many of those huge numbers were brought in for some kind of legal trouble or another, about something they might well have done and might not have had the slightest connection with . . . which never mattered . . . that poor was beside the point. Tillman could do all right on sheer numbers. He had gone over to their part of town and traipsed door to door leaving calling cards and assuring them if they were ever in any trouble to call him and he would see they were taken care of (knowing he might just as well have said *when* you are in trouble, for if the particular person he was talking to was not now or would never be, he more than likely had a brother or cousin or husband or wife who already was). And Tillman kept his word. He helped them solve at least their immediate legal problems, and Eunola's black people came so to believe in him that they would pay any amount, have any salary garnisheed, to get him to represent them. They called him by one name, what he was to them: Lawyer. Not Mister or Tillman or Hughes or anything added on, just Lawyer. Tillman liked that. The way they said it, it was almost like praying. The way they moaned. Lawyer, they said, help me, I am in trouble. In that way they talked. Oh, Lawyer, I need you, Lawyer. Not just saying it but singing, *praying* it. It didn't take much to rearrange and bend that Lawyer the way they said it, close it up on the end and turn it into *Lord*. Help me, Lord, help me. Like Jesus the son, the agent, interceding between mortals and God, Tillman, Lawyer, acted as intercessor between the black people and authority; and buffeted them from undeciphered punishment and unjustified maltreatment by translating court jargon and police ethics into their language, thereby making injustice automatically and magically explicable.

He was back in business.

But he wasn't happy.

Because he was not respected, and what's more, had no white clients at all. He was a nigger lawyer.

At night, in the privacy of his home, he railed against his new clientele. Blood vessels pumped faster, organs swelled up, bile collected, as over dinner he told his silent family what science had proved. He spoke of brains. African brains as opposed to Caucasian ones. Comparative weights, com-

parative sizes, comparative biological differences. He spoke
of "known facts" and superior races and inherent idiocy, ra-
cial retardation. Meanwhile waiting for the telephone to
ring, for someone white to ask him for something, to be
needed by someone white again. "It's smaller than a mon-
key's brain!" he screamed, as he listened for the sound of a
car in the driveway. "As tiny as this pea on my fork!" (Did
someone knock?) Afterward, in his sleep, Tillman had guilt-
ridden dreams filled with snakes and sudden calamities,
floods and fires and shameful sex acts with small boys made
public. Then, the next morning, he went down to his office
and became once again Lawyer. The Great Explainer. And
that was a lot to take, that seesaw, that tilt-a-whirl, that
merry-go-round, up and down and back and forth and
around and around, thinking one thing and living another,
never quite getting his mental interpretation of what he was
doing in line with what he actually was, yet never giving up
hope that his illusions and dreams would come round to
him. It took its toll. The hope more than anything kept him
on edge, just as the *almost* had, and soon he developed an
ulcer and a stone and high blood pressure, and his wife took
tranquilizers and his son unpocketed his switchblade and
rearranged his hair in duck-tails while his daughter's face
erupted in a siege of acne like a field of sulphur pits.

One day the schism between his life and how he saw
it, envisioned it, hoped it would be, was deluded into thinking it still might become, got to be a little too much to take;
that morning Tillman Hughes went downtown and before
his secretary got there very simply hanged himself with his
belt from the ceiling fan in his office. He left no note. Only
plaster all over his desk where the fan was beginning to tear
loose from the weight of him. A client found him. Three

people had to hold him down on the sidewalk to make him
quit screaming and tell them what he'd seen.

Tillman was buried in the plot he'd bought in the good
part of the cemetery where trees were. White people . . .
Methodists mostly, because they had fewer and less rigid
standards to uphold . . . came to whisper and look, while
black ones went to their own churches not to mourn especially but to regroup and figure out which way to go next,
now that Lawyer had gone off and done this.

After that his wife and children were treated quite de-
cently, as a matter of fact with even a good deal of respect,
once Tillman got rid of the evidence against them, his life,
testimony to their guilt.

As for the Young People for Christ-ers, they were long
since gone. They took their verse cards, their Bibles, their
posters and brochures and their decals saying "John 3:16
. . . BELIEVE!" and left town. Went north, where, it was
said, they belonged, and the YPC co-ordinator couldn't have
agreed with them more.

The saved youngsters wondered if it were all true, about
the card-carrying communists and all, but after a while, following the pattern set by their elders, they began to let go
of their dedication to Jesus and adoration of St. Paul, and
. . . once it left town . . . of YPC as well. And then, they
simply went on to the next thing, whatever it was, without
looking back, and being saved became last year's fad, a curi-
osity, from a new standpoint in time, looking back. It would
be years before they really remembered YPC again and the
interdenominational camp in the Rockies. As adults, they
would recall it and try to picture themselves making
campfire confessions and shake their heads at the memory,
wondering who they were then that they should come to do

such a thing and then lose it so completely. As if that sweet and committed girl or boy standing before flames were some dream of self, someone imagined, never real at all; and the memory something only read about in books, throughout the years coming to be thought of as real, but never actually having happened.

One thing they did keep because it was rote learned and too stamped-in to be forgotten was the word-for-word message of the verse quoted at every YPC meeting, John 3:16. Ask them now, they can still recite it.

You had to know how to behave, was all, and not *almost* know. You had to be able to recognize inside common everyday words and phrases; clues; hints. And knowing meant having lived in Eunola more than a little while. It meant family going back to where the knowing started and the clues were identified and the cryptic signals established. And if you didn't . . . you had to take the smallest smallest baby steps one at a time to learn them. (As Sexton had in his day. But few others since had his gifts and none that unlikely time.)

Outsiders had a hard time identifying those signs, because Eunola had a reputation for being a wild town, across the state and outside it, and strangers often thought there were no rules in Eunola what with all the drinking and partying and well-known cases of extramarital sex not only tolerated but condoned, justified. It seemed loose, too loose to strangers. Take the case of the constable: a man with a leg and a half, one chopped off above the knee. One lush and drunken night going sixty or more this man's car encountered a cement abutment and his right foot met his carburetor, inhospitably. This was a man who opened the *B* drawer of his office files every night at five and took out a fifth of Ezra Brooks, the empty of which went into the county trash box three hours later; a man who though seemingly sober during the eight hours he served Eunola never breathed a breath less than drunk the remaining sixteen: yet he was elected constable. Things like that puzzled outsiders. But Eunola had its rigid standards just as anyplace does, and Eunola took care of its own. You just had to be quick to identify who was who and what was what. That constable was a familiar institution to the white people of Eunola. Underneath his idiosyncrasies he was good folks, from a decent family, a man who after all needed a job now that his leg was cut off and where was the harm? The minute a YPC-er said "interdenominational" or—worse—"interfaith" and "we meet once a week for one hour in the homes of participants, take no collections, serve no refreshments, ask for no signatures," Tillman should have deciphered the message, decoded the end result: it was an oddity, it would not fit, and sooner or later it would violate some etiquette or other which would cause them to reject it and him too. It so happened that the one it violated was the one they felt most strongly about.

Only those with special dispensation escaped the restrictions of this rigid structure, those town characters who because of some quirk or lovable if offbeat trait were allowed more leeway than others and were treated like exotic relics brought back from foreign travel, the kind you put on a coffee table to show off and point at and use in telling about your travels.

There were others, besides Lolly and Booth and Alberta and Graham and Sexton, but these were not so high-blown, not dreams but only renegades from the code of decency and propriety the lack of which cost Tillman Hughes his respect and business. These characters were regarded lightly, with a smile and a hand brushed in midair as if to say oh, him, funny fellow. Nutty harmless people who added what is called local color; exceptions to the rule who yet had boundaries, who if they ever tried to use the circumstances of their privilege and position seriously in order to take advantage of the town's tolerance and good will would have found themselves in possession of new dispensations and rules, not so comfortable, which they knew very well.

Characters. Some, institutions even. Like Abe Hersch, the town's Jew Judge. Abe was regular and solid, not nutty or funny. Station and not personality set Abe Hersch off. When Abe ran for judge, no one else wanted the responsibility of arbitrating justice except an idiot redneck laundry truck driver from the other side of town. Faced with that choice, the electorate decided to give the job to the Jew, and as time went on they grew to appreciate Abe Hersch and even to be proud of him. Anytime the television cameras came to Eunola to ask about the civil rights issue people had Abe Hersch to refer to. Look at Abe Hersch, they would say. He never asked anybody for equality, did he? No, Abe *earned* it . . . now why can't these other folks follow his lead? Abe's name became a reflex answer to this kind of question. A good judge, a fair judge: Abe Hersch, Jew Judge, the best Jew they'd run across and by God *their* Jew and nobody better say anything against him or they'd find out quick enough how it went. And if Abe and his people weren't thought much of in other ways, were kept out of clubs and groups and the best cemetery, they would have to say Abe was fair, if a Jew, a fair Jew Judge.

Edwinna Mobley and Old Sarah, on the other hand, qualified as characters, funny, free people, maybe lonely people, who knew? Edwinna was from an old, established but no longer moneyed family, well thought of in Eunola's higher social circles. Her scoundrel husband, who crop-dusted and flew low for a living but high in life, had left Edwinna one night and not come back. And her with three children to support and no talent at all for getting up and putting on proper clothes to go to work on time each morning. So now Edwinna showed up at every supermarket opening or car unveiling, enlisting browsers and the curious to taste a new cookie or try a new mophead or sample a sausage or cheese spread. She gave cooking utensil parties and plastic container parties and even sold magazine subscriptions, the profits of which she shared with an organization to help the handicapped. And you couldn't get away from Edwinna when she was on a selling binge, she needed you too badly. If she ever saw you, you knew you might as well go on and taste what she was pushing and buy a box and get it over with because she was *not* going to let you go. And because everybody knew her and why she was doing what she did, and because she stayed within the confines of their definition of her as a nutty harmless woman of good birth who sold brooms and cookies to pay off bank notes, and because if she knew they laughed at her she never let on and never seemed to mind or take it seriously enough to make them feel ashamed, they bought from her in good humor and joked about it later. Every woman in town . . . and if you knew who was who and what was what you knew which women "every woman in town" included . . . once a year bought a pot or plastic container from Edwinna whether she needed it or not, to satisfy her own need for patronage and charity. If Edwinna knew they bought without need, she never said.

Old Sarah was the bootlegger. Her shack was on the county line, a gray weathered building no different from other sharecroppers' except for the traffic constantly buzzing. Her business boomed in every season, but Old Sarah's face was never seen. She was said to be a hundred and more years old and possibly was, for nobody could remember when Sarah had not been there. Now she was never gone. There was no time of day or night you could drive up and honk that Sarah would not respond. The gravel drive circled by the side of the house, where there was a single, glassless, shuttered window. At night it all but disappeared into the line of the house and a stranger passing by would have a hard time divining its exact location without some help. When the shutter opened, you yelled out your order, brand name and all, and within seconds a dark arm bare to the elbow reached out, palm up for money. A large wart hung by a thread from the tight dark flesh of her thumb . . . a hundred-year-old wart, it was said. Then, money clenched, the fist and arm went back inside, the shutter closed, and you waited for as long as it took her, sometimes as much as a full five minutes. If she didn't have your brand, she'd open back up and yell a short and simple "NO!" and you were supposed to name an alternate because it was assumed you didn't come all the way out to the county line to go niggling over brands and that you would sooner take anything at all than nothing, and if she did have your brand, the arm came back out with the bottle neck in its grip and you took it and left and that was it. If there was anybody else in the house with Old Sarah, nobody knew, but the shack was so well protected that robberies were practically unheard of. And the occasional bunch of kids who, having decided to go out and find out about Old Sarah, went knocking on her door were warned soon enough to get away, and strongly enough that they never came back to find out again.

Of course Old Sarah didn't own the bootlegger's supply. That—at the time—illegal but very profitable distributorship passed secretly from one white man to another. Whenever a man became suddenly and mysteriously prosperous and started building a new house or buying a lot of big new things, everybody knew he must have bought it, though he would never admit it. Then as soon as he'd made enough money to go into something else more respectable, say the lumber business or a car dealership, he'd pass it on and take his profits. Sometimes it even came back around to him, if he did less well in licit business. When the sheriff died, Old Sarah's place closed for the day and whether it was because she then had no protection, with all the police gone to the funeral, or because she was truly mourning, no one knew, but Old Sarah hung a large black wreath on the shuttered drive-up window the day of his burial.

Then there was Franklin Yu, Eunola's artist and a symbol of its tolerance for its Chinese population which . . . being back then cheaper and more expendable labor than blacks . . . had been drawn there by work building levees up and down the river some fifty years before, and was by now substantial. Franklin's graceful pen-and-ink sketches of magnolias and pale water color water lilies, along with his genteel temperament and inclination toward self-effacement, earned him a Garden Club scholarship to the Art Academy in Memphis. But every six weeks Franklin had to come home and paint more magnolias and lilies for the club and give a talk on art or his career or the gardens in Memphis. The ladies adored Franklin's sense of gentility and gratitude and because of this he was given special dispensation by them from his Orientalness. He was an artist, not a Chinaman. Or not one *first* anyway, which was something. He, and the other Yus, and the Lees and Lows, the Chus, the Wongs, Chows, Lous, and Lums lived quietly and with dignity just this side of Central Avenue, which divided Eunola's blacks from its whites. The Chinamen, people said, were all right; the truth was, they had not always been all right but over the years had become that way by keeping to themselves and operating decent family-run stores of one kind or another in their own neighborhood; by keeping those stores open on Sunday so that if anybody across town needed to buy something or cash a check, the Chinaman was always available; by their kids doing so well in school; and by being always clean . . . but mostly, by staying to themselves.

But the most famous of Eunola's characters was Rose Leuckenbach: Rose Foundations-in-the-Home Leuckenbach.

Rose had in her time hitched up more sagging Eunola breasts and trussed more herniated Eunola groins than anyone would ever admit or care to know about. Private Consultations in the Privacy of Your Home her sign said; her calling card, Rose Foundations-in-the-Home Leuckenbach. On her rounds Rose rode a three-wheeled cycle with a built-in aluminum trunk fitted on the ledge between the two back wheels. The tricycle was silver, and Rose rode it through town as if it were a fancy car, signaling turns, ringing both

handle-bar bells at once, daring anybody—with severe looks
and meaningful gestures—to ignore her right-of-way or steal
her parking spot. Rose was a familiar sight to early risers in
Eunola, for her day started at dawn. And when she wheeled
in for the night, her battery-powered light showed her the
way through dark streets. She had plenty of customers, so
she could make her own hours, for Rose was, like a good
maid, passed on from one to another. Every morning she got
up, brushed her hair back as tight as it would go without
distorting her face and caught it and shaped it over a
doughnut chignon, then hitched up her own waist-length
breasts, put on her brown gabardine suit, laced up her Red
Cross oxfords, and set off. And the calves of her skinny legs
were like hard knots in a shoestring.

Rose had a way of never looking at breasts and other delicate body parts her products manipulated that people just
naturally appreciated. She could measure and adjust and fit
and all the time seem blind to what she was maneuvering,
her eyes deftly skirting large weary nipples and sagging
scrota . . . both and any of which she referred to as "our."
"Let's put ourselves down into this cup just so," she'd say,
getting the customer to shake his or her protuberance into
the hardness, "and see if we don't have a *fit*." Her hands
were small and agile and managed these executions with
quick finesse; before a person knew it, he or she had become
fastened into a product without a moment's shame or em-
barrassment.

Rose rarely smiled. As she took her business and her life—
which as far as anybody knew *was* her business—very
seriously, she seemed to find little to smile about. Only
inches interested Rose Leuckenbach: certain numbers re-
quiring certain amounts of squeezing, lifting, manipulation,

or support. Only that. There were no special or unusual pre-
dicaments, there were only inches. Her job was to rearrange
them to order.

Her aluminum trunk, padlocked, contained the tools of
her trade, and Rose carried the key to it inside a special-
order pocket in her special-order bra, because, Rose thought,
you couldn't be too careful these days, you never knew
who might be after what that you didn't want them to have,
and Rose had some reason to know. Inside the trunk were
measuring tapes, order pads, catalogues, pencils, pencil
sharpener, samples, and a red and green pincushion shaped
like an apple. All these things were stacked in neatly separated piles, to give her easy access to whatever she might
need at any moment. And she had samples of so many kinds
of bras you would think there was not another different one
anywhere in the world. She had bandeau bras and waist-
length bras, hipline bras, longline bras; bras in rayon or cotton or rayon *and* cotton; bras of elasticized latex, satin, lace,
or nylon; bras strapless or strapped; back-hooked, side-
zipped, or front-hooked for the fuller, less manageable
figure. There were boned bras, gored bras, elasticized bras,
and crisscross bras for lift and separation, some with cotton-
padded straps for shoulder protection. (And straps exclusively were padded, for Rose carried no foam, no falsies, and
no push-ups; she did not sell, she informed those who asked,
for cosmetic addition or substitution or for purposes of al-
lurement; that was the business of other people, not her line
at all.) There was only one bra with pads: the one designed
for mastectomy patients, with two guaranteed leakproof
inflatable pads to each purchase—one to wash, one to wear.
Rose herself demonstrated the technicalities of this particular bra. "There's no use," she told prospective customers,

"no use at all in our not being able to hold our heads up and go about our business like normal. It is simply a matter of adding back on some inches we have lost." And, *sweesh*, she blew up the pad, fitted it in the bra, laid it across her own substantial chest as demonstration, then left the patient to try it on for herself. "The inflation tube," (this was thrown over one shoulder), "is included in the purchase price." She had maternity bras and nursing bras with cups that unlatched singlehandedly to allow a mother to flip out a breast while holding the hungry infant. Also combination maternity and nursing bras for now and later. Foundations designed to support, lift, separate, and enhance mammary glands of all sizes and shapes and, as well, to relieve the pressure those glands, if heavy, might inflict on other body parts.

She had girdles: panty and regular, waistline or banded, brief, boy-length or longline, four or six garter, boned or elasticized, split crotch, laced or pull-on, side-zip, front-hook, with nylon, satin, or brocade panels for support and control. One girdle her older customers particularly liked was an old-fashioned pink brocaded satin longline lace-up with coiled boning and side hooks, which supported the back and controlled the flesh, and, at the very least, encouraged correct posture. One slump, and boning pierced the flesh; which was reminder enough.

To combine bra and girdle, Rose had her all-in-ones, which restrained flesh from shoulder to thigh with no unsightly bulge to interrupt the smooth flow of a knit dress. Boned, gored, and split-crotched ("so we don't have to remove any garment at any time until we're ready to undress," or, in other words, you could pee without stripping), Rose Leuckenbach's all-in-ones dammed up all flesh in that area and entirely suppressed any clever fat's runaway urge.

For men, she had waist and abdomen girdles of boned elastic; back braces; shoulder supports; protective knee pads. Also trusses with snap-open fronts and a special patented slip-resistant rubber truss for scrotal rupture. In the bottom of her trunk were surgical support hose—which she often ran specials on, with purchase—and for invalids who had lost control of elimination processes there were boilable Keep-Dri briefs and bloomers for men or women in nylon or cotton with removable liners and ten inner layers and nylon outer coverings. The men's version had a snap-open removable crotch. You could buy as many extra of those as you wanted at a reasonable price indeed.

Most of Rose's women customers were what she called the well-endowed, whose breasts seemed a measure of their authority, which was prodigious. PTA presidents, Garden Club officers, church tithers, choir sopranos whose vibrato shook the stained glass . . . all shopped with Rose at home and carried their leadership as they did their breasts, with outward and uplifted pride. Any time you saw a woman with high new breasts pushed up in ferocious points, or noticed one walking as if she had a string tied around her knees and what's more if you looked close enough you could see she'd lost the crack in her ass, you knew Rose had a new bra or girdle customer. Rose Leuckenbach lived in a rented garage apartment and kept her tricycle chained at the foot of the stairs which led to it. As she had had the business and the cycle when she moved to Eunola, nobody knew much about her, where she came from or who she was, and Rose certainly didn't offer any information. So Rose was "Oh . . . Rose . . ." a funny lady who seemed to have no friends, and about the only thing she was known to have said outside business was "Two pork chops, center cut, very thin please" to the butcher. Anything else, if anyone heard, no one repeated. And being "Oh . . . *Rose* . . ." she got away with a lot.

There was a definite ordering to all this, as precisely delineated as a cross section of the earth diagramed by a geologist. If you could see the town in layers this way, if it were possible to make a similar crosscut plug of the town itself, you would have a better idea how it worked day to day. The topmost layer, that one visible to the innocent eye, the one most commonly referred to as Eunola itself, like the topmost layer of dirt is commonly called the earth itself, would be made up of Cunninghams, Strunks, the doctors, lawyers, city councilmen, cotton brokers, Garden Club ladies, and Yacht Club members. Presbyterians would be there; also Methodists, Episcopalians, builders, brokers, and councilmen. These people thought they were the town— Eunola itself—that their standards held and would keep holding and that when they said *everybody in town* it would always mean what it had in the past; that there would never be a time that that statement would have to be qualified or amended to include some others they weren't used to including. And the only time they even noticed those beneath them was when one was noticeably quaint or queer or smart or useful . . . or caused trouble. Down there was the gravel, the grit: the Georgia and Texas Baptists, the rednecks, blacks, Chinese, Jews, Peaveys; the trailer people, river people; the Italians. (There was, however, a distinction here: it was always better to be anything other than black; that was a strict delineation. A nigger was something else again, and he or she—while included in this strata of the crosscut plug—also stood out from it . . . there was no confusion at all on this point.) The town characters were there too, at the gravel level, Old Sarah and Abe and Franklin and Rose . . . but they kept their heads at the upper-level people's feet and would not be shoved farther down. And deep down beneath them all, so far down the longest leg of the tallest one above couldn't touch an outstretched hand of theirs, at the boiling fluctuating core were Lolly and Alberta and Graham and Sexton and Booth . . . dreams. Feeding the others, they moved constantly, their daring knighthood and potential power a store of ecstasy so fearful the others did not dare embrace it but needed it feeding them all the same.

Those at the top, the businessmen who thought they were Eunola itself, saw their world through old delusions, as distorting as outdated prescription lenses. To begin with they were not in control of the town in any real sense, because of what had happened a generation ago, when their ancestors had chosen to throw in their weight with a dream . . . of the *chosen*. Of inherited grace and superiority, of fantastic properties genetically transmitted; an aristocratic ordering. And so—minimizing the day-to-day realities of business and hard bedrock needs—they had yielded their power to that area's notion of aristocracy, the planters: the Darcys and Paynes, whose aura hung over the crosscut plug like a god's care. And to complicate the delusion even more, those at their feet, the characters, knew very well what they were doing and used their dispensation to their own advantage and secretly laughed at those who granted them their privilege. Rose for instance, nights, still in the inch-adjusting business, because she was alienated and free from scrutiny, had great success as the town's leading kitchen table abortionist, removing *those* inches with all the expertise and indifference with which she maneuvered sagging scrota.

And Alberta, who egged on her white customers' version of herself as their happy whore because it suited her purposes, gave secretly to the newly organized black people's association, not for revenge, but only to keep the spirit and potential the white man had passed on to her and use the revenue gained to help revitalize her *own* people's potential and spirit, one for one. Edwinna Mobley, who was lonely in her part, more than sales and samples craved *skin*. But, knowing full well that with her plates and mops and plastic container-ware parties, she was a joke and that jokes and sex never went together in a man's mind, Edwinna had to equip herself to take care of her own needs. She had a complete set of electric and battery-operated masturbating devices, ordered from the back pages of the magazines she sold subscriptions to, and had cultivated her imagination, as well, so that on her own she could turn ordinary household utensils into instruments of pleasure . . . candles, rubber hose, bottlenecks, broom handles, children's rubber hammer handles. With each orgasm, Edwinna wept, not from shame, but from loneliness—missing the rugged crop-duster, whose violence suited her passion so well—and the foreknowledge that she would soon be at herself again and would afterward feel even lonelier for it. But she could not stop. As soon as she finished a session she began looking forward to the next, dreaming of what she might employ, what might bring her to that special blankness that for one instant set her free. (Though she never had the heart, once done, to repeat herself immediately, for as soon as the blank moment passed, she became aware of the tools around her, from which she had chosen, like a mechanic with all sizes of wrenches at hand, and this sight depressed her and robbed her of any will to get there again right away. Only later would the tools

lose their look of utility and slowly begin to take on properties of the fantastic and the erotic once again, and, freed,
Edwinna Mobley would start the world all over again.) The
Jew Judge, Abe Hersch, was eventually to side with the un-
derdog, when they had been so open-minded all those years
and not cast him in that role, and Lolly would come to disappoint. Only Franklin Yu was steadfast: he upheld his
seeming, and painted flowers for ladies until he died alone
in his beautifully decorated apartment.

VII

LOLLY

On his collar he wore a pin that dangled below the first button of his shirt. As he pedaled it swung. He never missed a Sunday, whatever the weather, because he did not know he had a choice; when Sunday happened, so did his ride.

When he got to where she lived, he leaned on his handlebars, resting from the long ride, and stared at the door she would come out of. He stayed that way a long time, not moving, his eyes steady and almost never blinking. He didn't call or make any motion to get her to come out but only stood and waited, so still he seemed frozen. Finally the door opened, and he stood straight, and she came toward him, baton in hand.

The topmost pin was a white disc imprinted with a red cross and some gold lettering. The next was a gold laurel wreath which encircled the white disc and was attached to it by a clasp. Hanging from the laurel wreath were four small gold bars, each secured by a small hoop so that the bars swung back and forth as he moved. A white pin for the first, a wreath for the second, a gold bar for each successive year; in all, six years' perfect attendance at Sunday School, a record. But then, Booth Oates had little else to do, and Sunday was what the rest of his week waited for.

He smiled when he saw her and something in his throat gurgled and flowed. Walking out, she began to twirl and talk, as always, her voice and the twirling seeming to start together and from the same source. Booth watched the silver circles she made and heard the light whispery stream of sound coming from her mouth and thought they were one, each deriving from the other and inseparable from it. He looked into the center of the turning and did not leave, concentrating on it, taken inside, not lifting his eyes while Lolly chattered on and on, her hands busily working the baton. Booth was the only person she really talked to . . . though whether she was actually *talking* to him or was simply thinking out loud while he was there she herself did not know. For whatever reason, she did go on in his presence. While making figure eights and lateral neck wraps, she spoke of girls at school and going steady, and boys who gave away their football jackets. Booth's head went back as she threw the baton in the air, spinning. Her voice went on, feather light, just as the touch of her finger had been on his shoulder when she greeted him. Booth blinked against the glare of the sun and the silver baton turning inside it. Then it came down. As she caught it, she was still chattering, saying how she could not understand the silliness of girls, how they giggled and flirted and acted so cheap . . . which was true; Lolly could not fathom how they could treat their lives with such seeming abandon and lightheartedness because her life, to herself, was so serious. Though she created mys-

tery, Lolly had no notion of it herself and did not understand the power of fear or love at all: you did what you had
to, and got on with it, it was all within your power to control
and order. Just like with the baton, it only took practice.
And wanting it badly enough. Booth kept looking into the
center of the movement, where it started and then blurred,
and he saw nothing but glory. Like the leaping of a flame
when a lighted match was put to paper, the twirling baton
connected with no explanation in his mind. It was magic,
pure magic. She was spinning silver out of the air, creating
miracles from nothing. And Booth, more than anyone, let
himself fly off into it, as the cool breathy whisper of her
voice kept him there, blissful, floating.

It stopped.

"I'll get us a drink . . ." and she went away. The door
closed behind her and then she was back with glasses of
lemonade. He saw Lucille's face, filled with anger, go by the
big window next to the front door, and ducked his head. He
felt her hatred every time she looked at him, like a hot wind
passing by.

Lolly had left her baton inside and now sat back on her
hands, her knees up, her feet resting on the outside rims of
her tennis shoes. She did not drink her lemonade right away,
but Booth gulped his down in one long swallow, then put
the glass aside and sat as she did, leaning back on his hands.
When she realized he had mimicked her she changed her
position, crossed her legs and turned from him. Every now
and then he did something that reminded her he was, as
Lucille kept telling her, Sunday after Sunday, an idiot. It
annoyed her. She turned her head from him, stirring the
lemonade with the tips of her fingers. Booth watched as she
began to move down inside herself and go away. She did

not speak at all now; the voice was gone and with it the silver magic, and the serious stillness of her face told him it was time to go. The stream had stopped. What he came for was gone. It was time he went to the next thing. Shyly, he gave her his empty glass and climbed back on the red Schwinn he washed daily and waxed every Saturday, and started toward the highway. He turned back only once, to yell in his wide open ill-shaped way, "G'bah . . . Lah-lee . . . g'bah . . . Lah-lee . . ." Then he wheeled onto the highway and was gone, pumping his way back five miles to Eunola, where his parents were enjoying their Sunday rest from him . . . though Mrs. Oates never quite managed to loosen herself from him entirely.

One Sunday Booth waited two hours for Lolly to come out. Leaning down on his handlebars, his eyes steadily on the front door, he stood blank and unbothered until it finally opened and Lucille stuck her head out and yelled "SHE'S NOT HERE!" then quickly drew back in and slammed the door again. Booth did not leave; he stood as he always did, looking and waiting. There was nothing else he knew to do. Even when Frank came out and said he should go, he still did not, not immediately, not until the regular time. *Then* he turned his bike in the direction of the highway and pumped on off. Lucille watched him, muttering under her breath, and while Frank said nothing, he did think it was rude of Lolly not to have warned the poor dumb thing, when she knew in advance she'd be gone. (Which would not have kept him away, because when Lolly saw him again and apologized for having neglected to tell him, he just stared at her and waited for her to go on and do what was next.)

A band contest was held every year for high school bands of three neighboring states, and while Eunola High rarely sent its musicians and twirlers, the contest this year was held in a nearby city, and so the band members had sold candy to earn bus fare to go. Lolly entered every twirling event. And won every one. No contestant from any town any year before had ever won as many awards. She was named champion in twirling, marching, air maneuvers, composition of routines, special effects, acrobatic twirling maneuvers, and double baton twirling. She twirled that weekend like an angel. Slim rubber-tipped batons one at a time, two at a time, even three—one constantly in the air like a juggler's plates. She twirled fire batons, heavy steel batons, drum major batons as long as her legs. Holding a fire baton in each hand, she bent herself backward and kept the flames whirling as her head came between her legs. Hand to hand, around her waist, through her legs, between her fingers, under her armpit and over her shoulder in one twist, bounced off the ground, thrown high over her head— wherever it went, whatever she did with it, the baton seemed an extension of her finger tips. Other twirlers were proficient, maybe had comparable skills, but no one else had the rapport she did with what she was doing. Time was hers. Committed, she was one with the twirling. And she threw her baton, and caught it, and marched with her knees popping straight up and down and her back arched back as if it was rubber, and twisted her butt up and down the field, glittering in the field lights like a gold coin flipping . . . and the judges surrendered. They hated to give so many awards to one person, it was bad policy, but they had simply never seen anything like Lolly Ray Lasswell before, and since she was a senior and wouldn't be back next year, perhaps to embarrass them by doing this well again, they gave her the whole thing, right in her shiny gold lap.

Lolly responded coolly. She had performed well and knew it; she expected no less from herself . . . watching; all the while watching the silver stream or fire stream the batons left behind, feeling as if she were performing in a different world altogether, not a football field at all but some other, finer place. She saw no one while she was at it, only the lights.

Dauntless James Blue, as determined as ever, had convinced Frank it was safer for him to drive Lolly home than for her to wait around two days for the band contests to be over and ride home on the Greyhound she'd gone over in, and so he was in the stands applauding as she gathered up her trophies. He was taking her home. They were to leave as soon as she received the last one.

And while Frank didn't tell Lucille he'd allowed it, she found out anyway and before he could fend her off, scratched his face until it bled.

Having decided the time was ripe, somewhere between her triumph and Eunola, James pulled off the highway onto a lonely gravel road. Lolly was still flying from her victories, which he only sensed because she in no way shared them . . . and with all the excitement galloping around inside her, she ought to be ready . . .

She didn't want to give him any of her glory; after all she had earned it, and it was hers. But with happiness blowing up inside her like too many balloons and what she dreamed of almost in sight . . . her statue, her commemoration, *being there* . . . her skin could not contain the excess; it had to go

somewhere, outside herself. If there had been anything else
. . . but there wasn't and so she took what James Blue
offered.

She didn't feel much. It *wasn't* much, she thought, nothing like what she had imagined, especially with the window
roller pushing into her head and one knee slammed into the
ashtray and the other into the scratchy upholstery, and him
so heavy on top of her and her wondering if a car would
come by or some strange wild animal or the police, and . . .
had anybody ever been so close to her before? He was doing
strange things and making strange sounds, none of which
she could identify as the person James Blue or any other
human being she'd ever come in contact with. Really, it was
such a little bit of something to be happening to have been
made such a fuss over. Except for the discomforts, which
were decidedly *not* small, and the overall peculiarity of it.

At some point, she stopped him by holding his shoulder.
"James," she said, "what about . . ."

But she had asked at an inopportune time and James Blue
managed to say nothing, though he tried, then pulled himself out just in time and after a minute, told her it was all
right, she was safe. None of which Lolly understood, none.
Had he? Would he? Did he? And if he had, where *was* it?
And if it was . . . then when? All she knew was she ended
up a mess with some cold mucousy stuff stuck on her from
her navel down and . . . was that it . . . *the* it? Frank had
told her the essentials but this was different, something altogether very puzzling and strange. A whole new addition to
her experience of the world. And a substantial diminishment
of its potentiality.

All in all, she thought, it didn't compare with some other
things.

Still, after they got back to Eunola, she and James Blue
continued doing what they had started. Usually they went
to the cemetery because it was secluded out there and
James knew if anybody saw Lolly in his car he'd be in for it.
This reason he did not of course share with Lolly. It's quiet
out there, he told her, with only Sexton to see us, knowing
she liked it better outside than in the car. But when
mosquitoes were bad, which was getting more and more
often as summer came on, Lolly and James stayed in
his car and sweltered there. And James came . . . either inside those queer discs he bought or on her belly, his penis
throbbing lonely there . . . again and again. They became
chummier with Sexton after a while and James was able to
laugh about his first encounter with the knight; now he
could laugh about it or do anything about it, now that he
had her going. Lolly just about memorized the inscribed
poem, and they watched as the cotton stalks sprouted and
grew and made squares all around them, as they groped and
he panted. James left many a stretched-out rubber filled
with his sperm in that fertile soil; they formed a kind of
necklace around the oak tree's base. Birds pecked out shreds
to use in nests, owls dropped shit on them from their
perches. Rats stored bits of them as if they were valuable. They curled up in the heat and began to disintegrate.

The prospect of doing it, the secrecy surrounding it, were
always exciting to Lolly, and once they started, it seemed to
be simply what they would do at the end of a date. Just as
they had once gotten milkshakes or sundaes from the Dairy
Delite, it was a habit. And as Lolly had natural physical skill
and grace, she quickly learned what needed doing as well
as it needed to be done and as well as a person her age and
temperament could understand.

She learned to avoid the window roller and to keep one foot on the car floor to keep from rolling off. She learned to wear full skirts on their dates and girdles with a split crotch, and to keep her purse filled with Kleenex. She learned to tell lies more and more daringly and to move up and down instead of side to side or around and around as she had thought would be the appropriate direction. She found out how to say "having my period" to a man and how, when it was that time of the month, to get him to the point of making those strange sounds with her hand. (She never looked but just went at it, up and down and up and down until he reached for his handkerchief and covered the end of it and made the strange sound . . . but it tired her arm terribly; sometimes she switched back and forth from one hand to the other to ease the ache.) She learned she was supposed to like it when he sucked her breasts (he called it kissing, but she knew kissing from sucking, and what he did was suck) but never really did; in fact, she never learned she was supposed to go off inside herself, or could, like he did, or make the sounds. Nobody had told her it was available and she was too conditioned for simpleness to find out on her own. Her body gave her no information; she had lived in dreams too long. So she held on to her own version of the thing, while he kept on doing whatever it was he did. (Sometimes when he put his hand beneath her underpants, just laid it there and left it awhile, she felt something happening, a warmth, bright around the edges, but he always started moving it too soon and too strong and when he put the other inside her, she only waited for him to finish and felt little . . . except a kind of breathless sense of power that he was so affected by her.)

But she learned these things on her own, and never

asked James Blue what to do or how or if he liked it or how it was or should be and never said how it was for her, though after a while he certainly knew well enough. Just like Frank, James thought, never gives anybody the time of day unless he's pinned down and asked . . . and he was *not* going to ask. James knew better . . . she would say what suited her, true or not. He never really knew what was going on inside Lolly's head. She was so alone with her successes and failures, not even the crowds moved her. It was as if she turned another baton inside her head, one nobody else could see or touch, one she would not share. If it turned well and she caught it properly—which you never could tell about from the outside, for it wasn't simply a matter of dropping it or catching it; there was something else, a stricter set of standards she went by and set for herself—she was pleased; but if it went crooked or if she mistimed something or lost the rhythm, she was glum . . . she had failed; the world was dark and hostile. No one could reach her, James came to realize, because she had it all inside and after a while he quit even trying or thinking about it. But what he could do . . . with her, to her . . . he continued to, until after a while he began wondering how he was going to get out of doing it any more.

Lucille saw through every lie. Not constrained like Frank by any sense of moral duty to a prearranged code, she whispered under her breath to Lolly when Frank was out, said things to her Frank would have been shocked to hear. She would do anything to pull Lolly away, out of the direction she was going, anything, which included making herself more ridiculous than she already was . . . what difference did it make now? Down inside Lucille was a dark pool of knowing which she had no skill at using or communicating.

This information, she was positive, was right; she never doubted it. Only the way it came out, it sounded worse than she meant it to, and people were always shocked. The pool boiled inside her constantly and when she saw Lolly darting into the trailer after a date, it was stirred up, as if a stick had been poked into a swamp, churning up secrets. What came out of her then came straight from there, and was hateful, unadorned, raw, not made up properly for the outside world. "Girl," she whispered, "he's sticking it in you, I know he is. Isn't he, girl? He's the one with the baton these days, isn't he? Better get it out, Lolly, or you'll find out what's what, miss twitch-twat, born to squat. Do you? *Squat?*" God, her tongue was foul but she couldn't stop it or make it respect boundaries. She said what she had to, unafraid of consequences, or of Frank, from whom she was safe. Lolly would never tell him she was doing it; Lolly was afraid to. She whispered terrible things to her daughter in the dark, making foul accusations, keeping herself in control until Lolly ran off to her room and shut the door. Then Lucille's head went to her knees and she felt the collapse within her chest.

In June, the town announced its intentions regarding Lolly: they were going to send her to college.

Six men met privately and drew up a contract she was to sign if she accepted the money they had donated, which was enough to cover four years and would be given to her in eight equal installments, one for each semester. There were four stipulations: first, she was to pass all subjects; second, she was to continue to perform, in the state university twirling squad; third, she would return to Eunola to twirl at their

Homecoming games; and fourth, she would remain unmarried. Granville Stark, president of the bank, cleared his throat and made the suggestion for that last provision. "We do not want to face the risk of having a good-for-nothing husband slide in on her shirttails . . . or in this case, skirttails," he explained. The other five men agreed and the contract was delivered with the suggestion that she think it over before signing it.

Frank, still clinging to his trust of her sense of decency and self-respect, unwilling to impose judgments, said it was up to her. Secretly, he thought it was a good idea for her to get away from James Blue and besides, a college education wouldn't hurt, but he hated to see her tied to baton twirling for another four years, it was so useless. Lucille ranted so much about how she should go, make her, tell her she *has* to, that Lolly almost didn't to spite her. Also, there were her dreams . . . this wouldn't help, it would just be more of the same, more clubs and football games and crowds and books . . . even though she didn't know exactly what it was she was working toward, she knew college wouldn't give it to her. Sometimes she thought it was being Miss America or a movie star or an airline stewardess or being married to a rich man who would give her everything. But none of that was clearly defined, all she knew was it had to be something permanent, something which would establish her securely, and then she wouldn't have to twirl or turn or do anything but just stand there to have them all come to her. Like Sexton. All she would have to do then was be who she was, Lolly Ray Lasswell, *the* Lolly Ray Lasswell, of the world somehow, and that would be enough. There had to be something like that. Something that, once you got it, never let you down; something that made you feel you had stepped up as far as you could go. From then on, you would be, in your own eyes and everyone else's, *there*. You would have arrived. Like the Ivanhoe statue, she would simply *be* . . . yet have it all.

But she hadn't made a definite decision about any of this and so Lolly accepted the money and the stipulations, thinking she could always change her mind later and give it back if something better came along. And James Blue, who after three months of struggling in the car and the cemetery, crowned by a chigger bite inflicted on the tip end of his most sensitive part, who was ready to go on to something a little more comfortable, a little less hurried and rural—like a bed and, perhaps, his own wife—said it was a good idea for a person to get as much education as possible. Lolly smiled thinly when he said that, and they watched as each drifted away from the other and what they had had and were, without even saying goodbye . . . they just floated off away from one another and each went in a different direction, as easily as that.

Merchants laid gifts at Lolly's feet: a baby blue electric blanket and matching sets of sheets and towels, a clock radio and alarm, three pieces of tomato-red Skyway luggage, a fitted case of Merle Norman cosmetics, which was all the rage at the time, a gold-plated pen and pencil set, skirts, sweaters, loafers, and a robe . . . furry. Buddy Byars, the jeweler, gave her two sterling silver heart-shaped barrettes with LRL engraved on them, and Sam Pitts, the dentist, gave four years of free dental service, not including major replacements and repairs. Not to be outdone, Vale Batson donated the mandatory physical examination, including blood tests and chest X ray. As with all young girls going off to colleges and camps, Vale discreetly skipped over breast and "female" examinations and automatically checked "normal" on the sheet. Vale got a lot of business that way. Knowing that neither they nor their parents wanted young girls poked or punched in places they ought not be poked and punched in, Vale accommodated their wishes, and the word was passed on.

She was like a bride. She was being married to the whole town. There had never been so many big cars in the trailer park before, as people came out to bestow their gifts, each of which was duly noted in the Eunola *Enterprise* until the list became almost like a fund-raising contest to see who could give the most, the best, the most unusual. And Lolly . . . playing it out to the end . . . blushed each time they came, as deeply as a bride should, and dipped and sighed and quietly exclaimed, shaking her mud-rust hair from her eyes, "It's beautiful, thank you." Lucille stayed in the bedroom muttering, and Frank scowled each time he came home to find more gifts laid out in Lolly's room. But she was so thrilled. She brought things out to show him, and her eyes shone like her gold sequins, and he could deny her little, this least of all, this exultation. And so he said nothing, and agreed with her that, yes, it was all beautiful.

Frank himself drove her to college, refusing to let the mayor, who had wanted to. She immediately won a place on the twirling squad, was in fact one of the two featured twirlers, an honor never before won by a freshman. A prestigious sorority invited her into sisterhood, on the chance that her possibilities for campus acclaim might outweigh her poor family background. She had made acceptable grades by the time she came back to Eunola to twirl at the Homecoming game and made a name not only for herself but for the town as well, as the story of her twirling and the town's generosity had been printed in the newspapers of several of the state's larger cities. Lolly was a star; Frank and Lucille were absorbed into the silence created by her absence; she was representing the town honorably. Homecoming would be her first trip back to Eunola.

VIII

LADY

His interest in the race had paled. It was juvenile to go out and do the same thing over and over again and besides, the young boys and their girl friends bored him. He did not feel young himself; his mind was elsewhere. Here. Home. On her. Every day he watched what she did. Drifting by with her paperbound books. Staying in her locked room for such long periods of time. Watched over by Serenthea, who carried the key. Protected by Preston at night. He waited. His chance would come.

He sat in the dining room, out of sight. He heard Serenthea's steps approach her door from inside the room; their voices; the doorknob; the door. Then Serenthea's heavy tread, moving to the kitchen, glasses tinkling: Lady's breakfast tray. There had been no click after the door had closed. She had forgotten to lock it. Carroll waited until Serenthea was past hearing and the hall was quiet of her footsteps, then tiptoed to Lady's room. Silence. He hoped Serenthea would not suddenly remember.

The doorknob was cold. Pressing down, he turned it slowly to avoid a sudden click and gently eased the door open with the palm of his hand.

At first he saw only the back of her head, that glistening blond pageboy draped over the back of her velvet lounging chair (purposely situated with its back to the door so that she would never have to face anyone who entered but would always have time to collect herself, and re-create the mystery). He could hear her breath, rattling slightly. Her hair . . . so perfect . . . looked spun. Even in half-light it glowed. Carroll moved toward this, her head, the shimmering yellow flow, holding his breath to keep down the excitement flooding through him. He was close enough to touch her . . . she did not like being touched . . . close enough to make that choice . . . but did not, not yet. He would not rouse her or pre-empt his discovery but would let it unravel at a natural tempo. He would not force it. He skirted a small table beside her chair, barely missing its claw foot. She neither turned nor wakened. Her breath was mucousy, a light snore. He came round the back of the chaise longue, came quietly, slowly to her side.

Of all the rooms in the house, this one alone spoke wistfully of the past. Dark, oppressive, decorated with heavy Beall mahogany furniture sent from New Orleans at her request . . . the worn plush of velvet seats, the cool of swirled marble table tops, the gloom of huge beveled mirrors hanging like giant reminders, mirroring only darkness and half-light . . . these things created Lady's present, out of her past. His feet sank in her thick carpeting.

There was little light to see by, only that which came through a crack where the draperies met and left a jagged streak across her knees. But when he rounded the foot of the chair he could see what was in front of him plainly enough, light or no light, and knew then what she was. Sprawled on the crimson velvet chaise, her hair splashed over her now puffy face, her head thrown unnaturally back, the mystery book crumpled on the floor beside her, her gown pulled up in bunches, her hands curled like frail birds fallen from nests, her legs bent crazily, one bare foot sideways on the floor as if crippled, the other—slippered—against a knee, was his mother. Dead to the world. There was a small table beside her; on it was a silver tray containing a half-full bottle of bourbon, several glasses, a perspiring water pitcher. The rest of the room was in order . . . the bed tautly made . . . everything except her, Lady, the perfect preserver, exercising to keep her slim tan body in shape, her breasts high, her legs firm. Not mother, she had said but *Lady*. His mother nonetheless, in ruins.

Hearing him, or sensing his hostility, Lady roused, and turning her head, tried to lift it, desperate to continue her act. But her head wouldn't come; weighted, it only bobbled. Carroll didn't move but held his gray-green Beall eyes tight and hard onto her. Lady brought her knees up as if in protection and covered her eyes with her hands. What pale thin things they were, how colorless and dry, with what bright knotted strings beneath the surface.

She screamed. Her fingers were stiff. She screamed through them, calling for Serenthea.

But before she could get there, Carroll turned and walked out without saying anything.

Suddenly he saw his life take a new turn; he felt viable. Resourceful. There was something that had to be done that he was capable of, which no one else had been. Hers was a correctable state, of which he would be in charge. It excited him, as running the ten-miler had not; it was more daring, and he would be more filled up with it. Preston was wrong riding misfortune out, hoping for an upturn, a change in the weather. You had to seek out its heart and destroy it. You had to take control. You could not tolerate contamination, it would only spread and take over and leave you at its mercy. Lady had only misstepped; he would take on the responsibility of placing her where she belonged. She was his mother . . . this kind of behavior was not open to her.

He was not young. He did not feel young. Nothing had been allowed him as a child to make him feel gay or irresponsible. He had always had to check himself; think of what he ought to do, how it should be done. Now the feeling was outside him altogether. He would do what was needed without consulting inside himself. He would move outside that. As if this were a military maneuver.

Preston asked him to let it go and leave her alone, and explained as best he knew how things had gotten to where they were now, but when Carroll pulled himself up and said no, Preston didn't know how to refute his certainty. Carroll said she was going for a cure at a place in Arkansas called Bryson's, as if he knew more about her than Preston, and was that intimate with her needs. He had already made inquiries and found that it was expensive but good and had spoken with the admitting office. They were expecting her. All he needed was a blank, signed check.

Preston saw his own stubbornness staring him in the face. Maybe he knew . . . perhaps it would help . . .

"She has to go. It's the only way . . . whether she wants to or not. This is for *her*, in her own best interests."

Preston signed the check.

Four of them went: Judge to drive, Carroll on the front seat beside him, and Lady and Serenthea in the back, one from all outward appearances quite composed, the other gently sobbing. Crossing the river, they saw how bleak it was, how gray and heartless . . . the air was dry, smoky; leaves were beginning to shrivel. It was an early fall day with death in its core, a good day for Lady. It gave her something to move against, to keep her back strong and up to the trip and Carroll's challenge. Sitting in the moving car, speeding across the bridge, she felt stopped, removed from this place and time. She moved, in space went as the car did, but something else in her did not, and she felt as if there were no car beneath or above her, nothing holding her up. Only the truth of her own body, suspended, in a sitting position, alone. The entire trip, nothing came to tell her that that was a wrong impression, nor gave her the sense of being with three other people around her in time and space.

On the other side of the river, after another stretch of flatness similar to Eunola's, they came to some hills and then, before reaching the mountains ahead, they were there.

Lady walked into Bryson's without looking back . . . having never said anything to Carroll since he made his grand announcement nor glanced in his direction from the time they got her ready to go. She only squeezed Serenthea's hand and told her not to worry, then went where they told her to, and the last they saw of her was her back, beneath the fur stole proud and stiff, as she disappeared down the hall with a male nurse's hand firmly on her elbow to keep her from wavering. Her pageboy spilled down her back, flawlessly done, brushed and turned under by Serenthea for the trip. Her exterior was correct. He had challenged her for power . . . she would give him no easy victories. Only her hands, had she taken them from her coat pockets, would have revealed her terror. They trembled violently when she unclenched them, and were as cold as tiles.

It was night when the three crossed the bridge again and the river was beautiful. Lights from barges ambled by . . . it looked peaceful from that height . . . and the bridge inside the steel girders was lit up brighter than day. Going through it after being in such darkness was like waking up inside the heart of a dream, before the crash or the fall or the end or the final illumination, exactly in the center. And then they were on the other side and it was dark again.

For the first time in his life, Carroll thought he could see his future coming together and, like the road ahead, taking direction.

IX

WAITING

Frank Lasswell, driving through town, stopped at a red light and thought again of Lolly. Every time he was there he saw her and the shadow of her shadow, twirling and turning and dancing in the street, the sun glinting off her lithe sequined body, sparkling so it hurt your eyes to look, gracing their lives with light, tossing her baton as high as it would go, then waiting for it and, finally, catching it as she chose to. Dwelling in the past was foolish, a thing he did not believe in; nevertheless, he did it, time and again, endlessly recapitulating and remembering, trying as he went to clarify the memories and keep them precise.

The light changed and he went on, looking ahead. Someone in a truck passing by, going the other way, waved in greeting, but Frank did not respond.

He was the same. Life had not changed. Things went on. Only he hadn't known he would miss her so. Just that. Now that she was gone, the trailer seemed as big as a ballroom, the way he and Lucille rattled around in it. They hadn't found a way to live together without her, were at the same time too close and yet so far apart they could hardly find one another, with the boundaries so stretched out and definitions so obscure. Without the punctuation of her comings and goings, their lives went on and on and each day seemed longer than the one before.

Past the stores and the tall old houses that were Eunola's oldest, Frank turned right on Hawthorne, crossed Court, and went down some narrowing side streets where small neat houses appeared, lining the street one after another like small obedient children put in a row by a teacher. With well-tended yards and screened front porches and no curbs at the end of the yards but small drainage ditches along the street, these were the homes of Eunola's white-skinned working people. A neighborhood Frank would probably have lived in if he hadn't chosen a trailer instead.

He had just finished a day shift after voluntarily working another eight hours before that. He stayed away from the trailer as much as possible now.

Frank turned into one of the gravel driveways and drove on into the garage next to another car. As he went out, he pulled down the doors and shut them behind him, as she had asked him to.

(Mrs. Pope said that while she of course didn't really care who knew he was visiting and wasn't ashamed of it, she did after all have her reputation to think of now that she was alone and if people got to thinking about her *that way* why then every Tom, Dick, and Harry who came in the café would start thinking he was free to come by. And so Frank

closed the doors to the garage and always came in as unob-
trusively as possible, though he was certain her neighbors
already knew.)

Before he could turn the back doorknob, she was there,
panting with fat and excitement and good simple warmth,
saying wasn't it a simply *gorgeous* day! She was always glad
to see him.

Mrs. Pope's husband had worked with Frank. When three
years before he'd suddenly died, he'd left her with substantial insurance, no children, and an emptiness where her life
had been. Now she only went to church on Sundays and
Wednesday nights—thank goodness, she often said, for
church!—and to a knitting class Sears gave on Tuesday eve-
nings, though the only thing she had created so far was a
long trailing muffler she couldn't seem to bring herself to
finish. It went on and on, bunched up in knots here, loose
and saggy there, speckled like her linoleum floor. She
watched television and kept house, planted a few packets of
flower seeds in the spring but only got the zinnias to bloom
and they weren't so pretty. A cat had come by for a time,
then left, but she wasn't unhappy that she could say; she
didn't need much. She had taken the job at the café as much
to have something to do with herself as anything. She was a
waitress there, at Jesse's. Frank had met her over hamburger
steak smothered with onions.

They sat at the kitchen table drinking coffee. The table
was gay, expectant, with a bright yellow cloth on it, set with
a vinegar and oil cruet filled with plastic flowers. Mrs. Pope,
still wearing her orange nylon uniform and her hairnet, sat
waiting for Frank to open up the visit, not saying anything
until he did but about to explode with a story from the café.
She had been home awhile; the house was aired and the

kitchen straight. The house, utterly quiet, was much like its lone inhabitant . . . simple, pleasant, and squat, with a low sure pulse and clean corners. A pile of dishes lay in the drainer covered with a dish towel. She had barely had time to get them done before he got there.

When it was obvious he had nothing to say, she began to talk, and Frank watched, pretending to listen, waiting for her to be finished. Her hands were plump—fat, actually, she was fat all over, and had curly peroxided hair and a round face—and she moved them constantly as she spoke, in illustration of the story she told. Her fingernails were bitten to the quick; the tips of her fingers round and tiny, like her feet. All the weight was in the center of her: by the time it got to fingers and toes it seemed to have played itself out. She went on and on, chattering, her hands fluttering, drawing circles, flicking the air, lying flat for a moment then rising frantically again, like startled birds. They were small and delicate and hysterical.

When the story was over, Frank downed the last of his coffee in one gulp, got up, put his cup into the sink, stretched and said, "Well . . ." and went off to the bathroom and that was that.

He stayed long enough for her to get undressed and jump into bed, covered to the chin. A robe lay across the bed at her feet where she could reach it handily when they were through. Waiting for him, she suddenly realized she had not removed her hairnet and quickly stripped it off and fluffed and primped her short hair, pushing it up from the neck to give it shape. When Frank came out of the bathroom, the door of which opened into the bedroom, he was undressed down to his shorts, still smoking his cigarette, which he finished sitting on the side of the bed with his back to her.

After snuffing it, he lifted his bottom high enough to slip his shorts down, then let them drop on the floor and got under the covers and turned to her.

Fat. Like soft and grainy boiled potatoes.

She turned as he did and he fell against her large soft belly, which with a gentleness he was not accustomed to pillowed his loneliness. Absorbed it. Took him in. So simple. So much Mrs. Pope! He felt the shiny pliant fatness of her thighs; separated them; felt the cool pastiness of her breasts against his hard chest; her damp shallow breath crooning in his ear, a slight wheeze. She pressed against him and shuddered, jiggling now on the tip of him, making high gasping sounds as if her breath might soon run out. Her fat was rippling and shining under the covers next to him, and all around him; he was surrounded. She snorted with the effort of moving her bulk up and down and he pushed steadily, concentrating on one thing, getting there. There. With his head buried in the bra-strap indentation of her shoulder, he pushed a little harder and a little slower and moaned slightly then pushed again and held it and again and did not move again and . . . that was it. (He had not lied to Lolly; that *was* that, as far as he was concerned: *it*. That one expulsion, that easing. Period.) Mrs. Pope did what she knew how to do, held on as long as she could, pushing back until she was sure he was finished, then rolled away and lay on her back and . . . finally . . . caught her breath.

When she thought she'd waited long enough, she got up, in stages. First she sat with the covers tight around her breasts . . . he'd seen them only once or twice, they were large white veiny things with pale indifferent tips fading into the white and pinhead-small nipples which did not harden. Lucille's were long and stubby, like pencil erasers. She reached for her robe, then—her back still to him, her white fat shining—put her arms into it. (She was so adept at this maneuver, it amazed him; though he had seen her do it countless times, still, it was wonderful; he still marveled at her grace and skill.) The instant she was up, her left arm was sweeping over her buttocks, smoothing the robe down pat before he could see a thing. A remarkable performance! Not a glance of her flat, rumpled behind. On her way to the bathroom, she mumbled, something about what she would fix him to eat, her mind already back on food again. She primped her short curly blondined hair as she went and then disappeared through the door, which she closed securely. Inside, she ran water loudly.

When he was dressed again, they sat, and with the radio in the kitchen window softly playing, ate, and drank more coffee, rounding out their small ceremony. Then Frank drifted off and went where he lived, down inside himself, and Mrs. Pope, taking his lead, sat quietly, staring into her coffee, making loud hopeful sipping noises to break the silence . . . for which Frank was grateful. He wanted to hear no more stories. He thought of Lucille—he always thought of her, she was never out of his thoughts—and as always, wondered what he was doing there.

He soon left—it was dark now—and Mrs. Pope stayed at the table, delicately scooping up leftovers, scraps of meat, crumbs of bread, bits of cake icing. Staring at a patch of spilled ketchup on the tablecloth. Sitting shamelessly naked beneath the bathrobe. And fat. Holding on to what little had been given.

Frank drove out 84. Once he was gone, his depression lifted and he felt lightened, as if he'd cast off some burden—

some weight. Going to Mrs. Pope's helped. It didn't change anything, but at least it helped raise his spirits for a time.

Lucille watched a suspense story about a prison breakout. A small table was pulled up in front of her chair and on it was a bowl of white ice cream, dotted with red. She held the spoon in her mouth until all the vanilla was melted and had slid down her throat, then bit into the sweet and tangy cherry. It was a perverse pleasure. She hated cherries; she loved them; she saved them until last.

The intensity of her headaches had eased somewhat now and she drifted in time as if weightless. Days came and went. She could hardly tell when she was sleeping and when not any more, things were so plain and leveled out.

The first time Carroll went it was because he believed the others when they said they had. And if they could, he certainly was not afraid to. With his aloofness and cool audacity, nothing frightened Carroll much. Life seemed one dare after another and he hadn't seen any so far he couldn't handle. But when he finally made up his mind to do it, one September afternoon when the others who had bragged of already having gone were still at school, he did sit in the Roadmaster for a good fifteen minutes not making a move toward going in . . . not actually *afraid* but then not exactly anxious to pursue it either, not yet. Especially since he knew so little about it.

Across the road from where he had parked, ragged children were playing on the front porch, swinging on the posts that held up the corrugated tin roof. While one child ran and hid, the others held a flop-eared spotted dog until they counted to some specified number, which he couldn't make out as their high, singsong enumerating ran together with no breaks or breath between and no distinctions one number to the other, no lips touching, no tongue marking stops. Then they let the dog loose to try to find the hiding child. The dog roared and bayed then ran around sniffing and wagging until he found the child and ate him up with licks and slobber. Though most of the children were of school age, Carroll was not surprised they were home, in fact, hardly gave it a thought. It was natural enough; they went when they had a mind to.

As he was watching, a barefoot skinny girl, older than the rest, came out the front door and across the road to where he was. Her tight pink sweater—speckled with balls of wool—barely reached the waistband of her skirt and her hair was done up in screws over her head. Frowning, she came straight over, across the soft pale dirt road, and asked him brusquely did he want something . . . which she already knew and what it was too; no white man ever sat in his car across the road from that house if he hadn't come for it. Carroll mumbled and nodded and—now that the decision had been made for him—swiftly got out of his car and followed the girl across the road to the house. She told him how much and took his money, then pointed him the way to go and left him there just inside the front door.

Though he was too old by most other boys' calculation and experience, discounting some fierce individual and group masturbation at school, Carroll was a virgin. He didn't know what was in store, not specifically. Carroll concealed this plane of innocence with aloofness, and sometimes when he secluded himself from others by putting on his mysterious, brooding face—which gave them the idea he knew more than he was saying—he was only doing it to give himself time and space for listening, so that maybe he could figure out what they really meant and how he should respond. They talked so freely and with such ease . . . of girls and dates and experiences in cars. How they could say it so nonchalantly and let themselves breeze on with such willlessness, to simply *feel* so effortlessly, was a puzzle to Carroll.

It was so dark!

Outside the sun was high, but here . . .

Something was cooking in the direction the girl had told him he was not to go, an unfamiliar smell, something rootish he thought. Carroll walked slowly through the front room to the door she had waved him to, feeling his way. It seemed to him that this was where darkness started, that when dusk came and the sun started dropping into the river, the dark of night would begin here. As though an invisible stored rug would roll from this room outside and over the land and across the river and into houses and around people, until morning, when it would roll itself back up and come to rest again in this small, very clean house.

He followed a faint yellowish light coming from down the hall. Standing in the doorway from which it came, he saw her. She was sitting in a big overstuffed green chair turned sideways to the door so he could see the side of her face as she smoked a cigarette and read. A floor lamp with fluted shade stood beside her and gave out a soft orange glow: warmth, pouring down on her head. The room was plain and clean; the floor was of unfinished planks of wood, scrupulously swept. There was an old mahogany dresser against one wall, with a large matching mirror over it, and a dresser scarf, neat, and starched ironed, covering the top. The bed matched the dresser and had spool-like posts at each of its four corners. The bedspread was white chenille, tucked properly under the pillows. All rather girlish and proper, as if some mother oversaw the tending. There were orangish window shades and lace curtains reaching the floor. She held the book in one hand and with a finger along the binding to keep it open shifted the book over, back and forth as she read one page and then the next, never cracking the binding, as if the book were something she would not treat unkindly. It had a paper cover, like the mystery books Lady pretended to read. Carroll had never seen a black person read a book.

Her hair turned in fat shiny curls, lying on her head like sleeping eels. Her legs were crossed; the top one swung slightly. She wore a black wrapper with a flowery print . . . large showy flowers, huge wide-open pink roses, big and heavy like cabbage roses, came out in soft bursts all over the garment. She didn't look up but, with a bemused expression on her face, kept smoking her cigarette, puffing it lightly, pulling at it in a way he was not familiar with. She held the cigarette between her thumb and first finger, which she had pinched together and pushed against her lips. Neither cigarette nor hand moved, but stayed in place as she puffed continuously, the smoke curling in and around her mouth, rising over her head, the stream gently moving, moving, never allowed to die. She did not drag on the cigarette but kept tugging at it, and the smoke drifted uninterruptedly into the fluted lampshade and came out the top so that the light in the room seemed itself to snake and turn.

She noticed him. She did not put down the book or her

cigarette but only motioned him to the bed with the slightest gesture, as if she had known all along he was there. As he made his way across the room, she finished the page she was on, marked her place with a matchbook cover, then laid the book on the floor beside her chair.

Summoning up all the Beall nonchalance he could muster, Carroll went over and sat on the edge of the bed across from her . . . not far, almost touching the top swinging foot . . . as if this were old hat to him too, as if, like her, he had done it hundreds of times before. She looked him full in the face, still sucking on the cigarette, her eyes almost closed as the smoke drifted in a sheet up her nose and into her eyes, like a screen of silk.

He had not expected her to be so black. Details in her face were undifferentiated, nothing was distinctive, as features melted into color and color was all. All he saw was blackness, screened by the curtain of smoke. She looked squarely at him as if to establish the fact of her darkness and give him opportunity to leave if he could not cope with it . . . as some could not. But Carroll didn't drop his head or lower his eyes, and so Alberta moved her hands up and opened her wrapper at the top to let him see her chest and great dark breasts, as dark at the chest as at the nipple, plumped out, lying placid on her midsection. And still she looked at him and smoked, urging that now-tiny butt to yield the last of itself up to her. She was giving him one thing at a time. A test to see how much he could take, how long he could go without blinking. So far he had not, he was passing so far, but it was not easy, not with her looking at him so straight in the eyes and the wrapper now entirely open and her body laid out in front of him, the texture of her skin so tight it seemed to be without pores: slick, tight

. . . you could bounce on it. Her navel went deep into her
stomach and seemed to stare too, like her eyes, daring him
to do it, do it, *blink.* Carroll thought for a minute he might
faint. He could feel cold and hot flashes alternating running
across his forehead, one saying first you, then the other
pushing from the other side saying it's your turn now, you.
Lord, it was not easy. Then she did a thing he'd never
have believed because Carroll had never run across a
straightforward woman before, one who looked at him
straight-on and did not dip or bow or turn this way and that,
silly and coy and evasive. He had never known a woman
who simply went for what she wanted and if it was to be
had, got it. Not until this one. Who did not choose to blink.

She mashed her cigarette—which couldn't have been more
than a quarter of an inch long—into a small amber ashtray
on the arm of her chair then reached over to him. His hands
were flat on the bed holding him up, marked in pocks by the
chenille. She took the one closest—cool, damp, bloodless—
and put it beside her knee on her leg and then began pushing it up her thigh, her hand on top to guide his and her
eyes still locked on his, wide open, enormously dark, as
knowing as if they contained all the mystery the world
never knew about. His legs opened; he wasn't sure he could
contain himself; it hurt. She moved his hand up, straight up,
not fast or slow, only catching on, Dynaflow-style, steadily
up her leg, like the Roadmaster cruising out at a steady honest one-fifteen, not pushing or straining but humming easy,
and he felt the pain harden to a solid throb, and as she held
him she watched him and still he held on, keeping her gaze,
not blinking . . . so far, containing the flush that boiled inside him. She closed her thighs softly together; they enveloped his hand, warm there where one had been on top of

the other, and took it between them like a secret they would not reveal. His hand . . . it was so near what he did not know, it would take only a mere stretch of his longest finger and it was his, he would find out and keep it forever. But he did not have to stretch or even move on his own, in fact he barely had time to think of it, because at that moment she, still taking his eyes straight-on as if knowing everything he was thinking and feeling, the knot of pain included, moved his hand up inside herself, guiding it right on up, and in, right straight on up into it. *It!* Whatever he had imagined it would be like did not come close; it was outside all imagining, that silky pearliness, that warmth and softness and firm muscularity, flesh like none he'd known or dreamed of, nothing like anything of his own at all . . . and not wanting to, Jesus, he did not want to and how he tried not to but how he was not able to stop it once it began, the push . . . he . . . *blinked.*

Right then and there, inside his pants. Closed his eyes and felt the deepest most hidden part of himself flow out in one unthinkable gush, like a little boy peeing in his pants in front of the classroom.

Carroll opened his eyes and found her still looking at him but with laughter in her eyes because of course she knew. Opening her thighs, she let him pull his hand out and as he was preparing to rearrange himself back into his solitariness laughed warmly then brought him back out of it, saying, "Son, that's the easiest five dollars I ever made!" And when she took him by his damp hand and pulled him down on the floor before her to let him find out what was really there, he was comforted, and began to learn.

Carroll got better at it—could go without blinking longer —after she taught him some, and after a while she said he

wasn't half bad for a white man. (He never knew exactly
how to take that, whether she was teasing him or meant it
seriously but he never asked because he expected it was not
a joke at all.) Carroll found at Alberta's what he hadn't
known existed, something he could throw himself into and
want badly enough to put his pride at stake in order to get.
He took money from Preston's wallet and even now and
then worked at the gin for wages, and crossed the bridge to
Arkansas looking for fresh challengers to entice to come to
Eunola and race the ten-miler to Sunflower . . . for money.
Preston didn't know what had come over the boy, and at-
tributed it to his taking a stand on Lady's going to Bryson,
and was glad to see at least a spark of life in the boy anyway, whatever the cause.

During the time Lady was gone, Carroll went to Alberta's
regularly, until Alberta became necessary. As vital as food
. . . not, however, like food for nutrition or sustenance, not
like what a starving child needs to simply keep itself alive.
But a hunger like that he felt for the food he was used to
at home, food for pleasure and lingering taste, the memory of which stayed in his mind hours afterward and longer,
weeks, even years—as the taste of ham in gravy, and cobbler
oozing fresh fruit became a sensual memory the very
thought of which brought back the taste. Richness. Deep
goodness. Mystery. A boy like Carroll was brought up to expect homemade hand-turned extras and for a boy like that
eating just to get full was like not eating at all.

He waited for Lady, who had a similar sensual spark,
buried beneath the aloofness, but, unlike Carroll, was afraid
to indulge it. She had done what she could to keep hers in
check, while Carroll pursued his, with all the doggedness of
Preston setting out to learn about the land.

Preston worked without letup, focusing his energies, as always, on what was to be done next. They were busy into harvesting; it was a good year. Nervous inside, he covered it over with dedication to tasks ahead. Something burned in the pit of his stomach . . . doctors recommended milk to cool its flame. He only cared for her. And the work. Everything else he could let go by, including his duties to the old women in the pink house. Nothing else mattered. Only that she stay, whatever the cost. He would never let Carroll override that need again. Never. He was afraid of what she would do to him when she returned—what it would be, he couldn't imagine—but something . . . she would find a way to have the last word.

Every day he was gone from the house by sunup and returned as treetops grabbed for the blood-red sun. He worked. Nothing else. And at night, when he couldn't help it, in bed awaited her return.

X

LADY

In mid-October, four weeks after she left, the director of Bryson's called Carroll and pronounced Lady cured. *Dried out* he called her, and ready to assimilate. He suggested some precautionary measures to take to forestall relapse. Carroll listened carefully then sent Judge and Serenthea to fetch her.

Preston and Carroll waited all that day as anxious as parents, Carroll sitting by the picture window long before the time she could be expected to get there, looking for the dust of an approaching car while Preston busied himself in the garage, pretending to tinker with one thing and another, also looking down the road. At dusk, the two of them sat down to a cold dinner Serenthea had left, and afterward went back to waiting.

It was dark when she made her entrance. She hadn't lost her talent for surprises, that was clear, because an entrance was what Lady made all right, and they hadn't anticipated it at all.

Lady came home dressed fit to kill.

New dress, new hat, new shoes, new gloves, new purse. A manicure, hair set and massage by a Bryson-ordered beautician. New perfume behind her ears. Impeccable and subtle make-up. Even a new, darker shade of stockings, held up by a new black lace panty girdle . . . though they'd never know. A new shade of matching lipstick and nail polish, appropriate to her richer skin color and the glow of health she had acquired from vitamin shots and timed sessions under sun lamps; appropriate also to her new single-mindedness: orange. More assertive, less wistful and dreamy, it suited her purposes. She was a picture, this radiant creature walking back into the Cunningham house like a queen visiting a colony, her servant Serenthea trailing behind like a part of her that had broken off and was trying to catch up and reattach itself. (The director had approved of her purchases; it was a sign of health he said—an indication of her new self-esteem.) Without a stumble or falter, she came back into their lives as she had left, with outward balance and grace and perhaps an even greater measure of serenity; her step a bit surer, her shoulders as she turned to greet them thrown farther back, her gaze less revealing than ever. Having slipped one more notch outside their world and the rigors of time and space it imposed, she told them nothing they wanted to know and allowed her eyes to yield no hints. Smiling, holding out a gracious hand to greet them, she was outside their control altogether.

She looked the way Carroll remembered her the times he came home from school—that slick and golden woman, immovable, preserved, beautiful—and now, intimidated by her composure, he felt shy again, and could only mumble how well she looked. But this did not last and soon he was gloat-

ing—after all, wasn't he responsible?—and clucking like a fat
hen. But Preston, where was he? There. Seeing the iron look
about her eyes, distrusting her performance, he stayed in
shadows, flapping and fawning like a trained seal begging
fish for tricks. He hoped this struggle would not last too long
or become too bitter.

Lady said she was tired and went to her room. There,
she went immediately to bed and soon, helped by a pill
Serenthea brought, to sleep. The costume show had been an
ordeal.

In the days following, every time they talked *to* her, they
talked *about* her. How beautiful she was, and how glad they
were to have her back, how much better her life and theirs
would be from now on. Carroll seemed to be working at the
office, in fact, seemed to be in charge altogether. He did the
majority of the talking. They had planned a trip, he said, to
an island with beaches and blue water you could see to the
bottom of . . . as soon, Carroll said, as the harvesting was
done and a certain contract finished and signed. They were,
he said, selling some land, acquiring some. Lady smiled
back when they said those things and tried to think of something to answer in return, but, empty, only smiled and nodded. Like a mechanical bird endlessly bowing.

They watched her so. Examining her every move, every
hesitation, stumble, her very breath. At dinner, if her hand
lifting a soup spoon trembled or if her neck shook a bit as
she bent her head, there was a sudden breathless silence as
they waited for her to go on if she could, to see if she had
perhaps relapsed, had, as they called it, jumped back in the
bottle.

"You mean so much," Preston said. He whimpered these days. What had Carroll taken from him? "All this," circling his arm, taking in everything, meaning . . . she did not know what, "is for *you*." He sounded desperate.

He tried to get her to tell him what she planned. There was something . . . he knew her moods if not her reasons. Something she was going to do. He wanted her to know what she meant, that he wanted her to stay, whatever the cost. Drunk or sober.

Biding her time, she performed. Smiled and made herself beautiful, keeping her purpose in sight. She asked Preston for a new car, which he immediately bought, despite his growing uneasiness. Carroll thought she was getting better and better.

He never saw her mornings when she lay for close to an hour flat on her back, arms stiff, looking straight up at the ceiling until Serenthea came in with a breakfast tray. And never saw Serenthea lifting coffee to her lips by the spoonful, feeding her the first few bites of food, until she felt strong enough to sit up and do it for herself. And never saw how she hesitated. How eating plainly disgusted her, because it was no good, it led to nothing except more of the same and only went on and on and when you finished for one day there it was again staring you in the face, the prospect of another and another, more of the same, more of the same, to which there was no point. How people did things day in and day out forever she never understood. But Carroll saw none of that.

She had nothing to move toward. The liquor had at least been that. Every morning, tilting in its direction, she had gone to it, calmed by knowing it was there. Now there was nothing, empty time, ticked off in chops. *Chop . . . chop . . . chop . . .*

Dried out? Literally. There was not a drop of moisture in her body and not one illusion to give her some light to go by. Her skin flaked like old glue.

She sat before her dresser, prettying herself up to go out and play bridge at a party she was certain Carroll had arranged for her to be invited to, in accordance with the clinic's favorite adage: when you get home, get out, go places, see people, get outside the walls of your own self-pity. Serenthea, also under orders, stood guard. Nodding in a chair, she was almost asleep.

She had at least discovered her reason for drinking at Bryson, or anyway one reason, whether or not it was the only one or if that even mattered. It was by accident, an uncharacteristic slip of the tongue. Before patients—or *clients*, as they preferred your being called—could leave the clinic, they had to get up in front of all the other *clients*, and tell why they drank and why they were stopping and what they planned to do now that they had. It amused her the way they said drink that way, with no object stated, just bald, flat *drink*, as if there were nothing else *to* drink except that.

She looked at her reflection in the great heavy mirror and smiled. None of it mattered now. Everything was a joke . . . a lark, like old times. It had all been settled, she had lain in bed planning it out, creating the next space of time before it came, so that there would be no shocks or surprises, and she would be ready and would not have to worry about losing the perfect architecture she had so carefully built. Lady. She would remain. Her way was clear.

The speeches were Lady's favorite entertainment at Bryson. There was always something amusing about them, something ludicrous, what with everyone being so serious about the listening and the making, and most of all the believing from both sides of the fence. She heard her first one soon after she arrived. It had been made by a repeater, a woman who had been cured once and was at the clinic for the second go-round.

The woman started off by telling about her previous stay and what had happened when she got home to make her start drinking again. (They all came back, either to Bryson's or some other institution; just like home, it was simply more of the same repeated endlessly.) The woman started by saying how hard it was "back there" to stay sober and how much her family had tried to help.

Lady chuckled softly.

Help. Who could help? Who could reach past a will so determined to have what it wanted that it would pay any cost, regardless of lives contributed or pain inflicted? Dressed in a navy blue satin slip edged in wide lace, she looked pale again, the unnatural tan having faded fast, the sickly pallor of exile having returned and with it, pale pockets beneath her eyes, melancholy loops, catchers of tears and sadness. Her shoulders were thin, and her collarbones protruded. Like sticks, she thought. Like thin brittle kindling, heaped up to start a fire larger logs would carry on.

The woman's family had written notes. "Little notes," she had called them, saying, "Please, Mama, don't drink." These they had placed all over the house, in cabinets, propped inside the bristles of her brush, taped to garbage cans, hidden in drawers and closets, stuck in mirrors, between plates, behind books . . . some of the same places she had once hidden liquor. Everywhere she looked there were more reminders, another note. The woman, whining, desperate to believe what she was saying, said it helped, she said it made her think of her three small children and how they felt coming home to an empty house while she was at the clinic or, even worse, to a drunken, passed-out mother, and how ashamed they must have been, and what a good childhood *she* had had in comparison, filled with friends and family dinners and fudge and popcorn in a warm kitchen. She said it helped to think of those children, who deserved better, writing such notes, begging her please not to drink.

Lady's skin was dull now and had no resilience or tautness. It was spongy. She smeared on make-up to fill up gaps and cracks and powdered it to make a smooth mask over the lifelessness. So many resources used up . . . so much gone by . . . She covered her stark thinness with a dark blue long-sleeved blouse ruffled at throat and cuffs and sat back down on the bed, staring at the closed silk draperies across from her. She still could not tolerate light.

After all the notes had been discovered and read and the woman had been home long enough for her family to come to depend on her—five months—the day came when she was sitting alone at her kitchen table, reading a recipe, feeling smug. The recipe was for a pie, she said—and she was very specific about this—a pie made with lime Jello and pineapple and cottage cheese, with a graham cracker crust. Sitting, reading, making a list of things to buy . . . crushed pineapple, Jello . . . when without warning, just like that, when she wasn't thinking of it or feeling bad or mistreated in any way, not unhappy or desperate or in the least a failure

. . . the urge came down, cracked open her head, and she wanted it. Again. And then it was only a matter of time. The rest of them at the clinic had leaned forward as she began to tell of it, how she felt it run so strongly through her whole body that she thought she would vomit with need; with her all the way, they fairly drooled hearing her say how it had come—just like that, she said, snapping her fingers. It was so quiet in that room the slightest ahem would have seemed an explosion.

Now how could an outsider hope to understand that? That it was bliss . . . and worth all the shame and condemnation? When they, the outsiders, could stand life without it? The woman said she had thought after five months sober she was cured, but suddenly it was back, the fancy for the taste, everything. Listening, Lady envisioned the woman sitting at the table reading the recipe, her eyes slowly lifting from the page, filled now with a dreamlike expression having nothing whatsoever to do with crushed or sliced pineapple, red or green Jello. She saw how angry the woman was, too—unknown even to herself as she sat thinking she loved them—toward her family and their notes and expectations and hints and offers of help, and knew the exhilaration she felt, getting loose from all that, her will running ahead of her while her heart yet held back, resisting, saying no, lengthening the anticipation, drawing out the preparation: where to go, what to buy, which glass to use, how much to pour, where to hide it, all the mechanisms of the act now taking on fantastic and powerful properties . . . how to do it . . . how . . . how . . .

The woman had looked so simple and dumb and doomed, standing in the center of them like a child on the first day of school telling how she spent her summer. And by some gorgeous and ridiculous stroke of fate, she had buttoned her sweater wrong. There she stood, her moment in the lime- light, weeping and wailing, with one end of her sweater lopsided beneath the other. It was the fine kind of detail Lady loved in the speeches; something like that was always happening to cut the dramatics and entertain her with a bit of soft-shoe irony.

Standing, she drew the black lace panty girdle over her hips and hooked stockings to its garters, then slipped a gray flared skirt over her head, careful not to disturb her make-up or hair. The waistband of her skirt drooped in front and hung on her rail-like hipbones as if on a hanger. Un- bothered, she hitched it up, belted a slim length of navy leather around her waist and sat back down.

Serenthea was snoring now, a deep rolling hum which filled the room with innocence. Preston gave her nothing useful. Only Serenthea, total good, filled her out and made her feel whole. If she could grab hold and cling, melt, stay . . . perhaps . . . but on her own she could never be more than a fragment.

As if sensing Lady's attention, Serenthea shook her head and, her large eyes blinking, came to, awakening as if start- ing over, reinventing the world. A new day.

Lady slipped her feet into slender kid shoes with a thin strap around the heel and began to talk. Her voice was tinged with bitterness now, overlaid with an irony floating in and out of the boundaries of sarcasm.

"Serenthea, did you know I made a *speech* at that place I went to?" She tried to hold her chin steady and to keep the corners of her mouth from turning down, the way Carroll's did.

Serenthea, foggy, didn't answer . . . frowned.

"Well, I did. I had to. Had to say to all those people there why I *drank*, though I didn't actually say that, *drink* like everybody else did, because I couldn't bring myself to. It, I don't know, sounded so tacky that I couldn't and so I only said why I *do* it, or *did* it, which wasn't much better I guess. Anyway, I had no idea what I was going to say but everybody was waiting and I had to say something so I did. It just sort of fell out before I knew it and I had to laugh afterward because it sounded so ridiculous and trivial and yet, the more I think of it, it seems maybe true, or at least partially. I said, 'I suppose I do it to shut out everlasting boredom and to keep monotony from taking over.' Just that. Do you think that's possible? It hardly seems so, it's so simple, like something Mother would say. Doesn't that sound like her? I remember she used to talk about tedium, or was it tediousness, I can't remember, but I don't recall *monotony* and now that I think of it I can hardly imagine myself saying it either . . . everlasting boredom and monotony taking over. Isn't it curious?"

Her voice drifted off. And what was monotony but time itself made too aware of, the tyranny of it when you tried to look too closely instead of living deep inside it, letting it have its way, going as it willed. You had to keep on; at some point you had to stop investigating and holding back in order to figure it out, or it would become unbearable. She had known that for years.

Serenthea, fully awake now, begged Lady to stay home. There was something about the way she talked that Serenthea did not like and she promised to lie for her and take the blame if Carroll found out.

"No," Lady replied with warmth. "Thank you, but no.

I'm going." And slipping into her suit coat, she finished her story.

"Shoot, Serenthea, I guess maybe I'm just jealous because my story wasn't as good as everybody else's. No fancy reasons. No husband beating me over the head. No ugly childhood. Why, my story had no punch at all, no pizzazz. Boredom! Well, I'm ready now. I'm finished. How do I look?"

Beautiful, Serenthea said, and though much of it was pasted together and held up by pulleys and pins to make up for gaps, she did. The eleven other women at the card party said they had never seen her more beautiful. And in days to come they would say how sociable she was that day, how talkative and normal and friendly, not like the old snobbish Lady at all. She even kept her mind on cards instead of making foolish mistakes on purpose to draw attention to herself, and laughed out loud at the honest mistakes she did make. Nobody remembered her being so outgoing before. She drank no liquor at all, though it was offered, not even sherry, and joked with the others about it, saying, "No, thanks, ladies, my son won't allow it and my son is very strict!" She did well. Because at last she had extra space in her mind, which allowed her some casualness about herself and the time to come and gave her ease in thinking what to say, instead of sitting tied up in knots wondering what was expected or, if she knew, flaunting disdain for it. The party went on all afternoon from one until well past five and Lady stayed until it was over because she was clearly the life of the party. The telephone rang several times and from the gist of the hostess's whispered conversation Lady surmised it was Carroll calling to check on her. But they were loving her so, she let them go on and on all afternoon. They asked

if she would join them for another party. Yes, she said, she'd
love to. And would she come to the Garden Club meeting,
the talk would be on azaleas? Yes. And play golf two weeks
from Thursday in the Women's Handicap? Yes . . . though
she couldn't promise how good she was any more . . . and
join them at a dinner dance next month in Memphis, she
and Preston if she could get him to go . . . oh, yes, yes, she
would buy a new dress, red . . . it was so easy to say what
they wanted to hear, she was saying yes to everything. The
other women were astonished. They followed her out to her
new car to inspect it, it was a Thunderbird and didn't they
all love Thunderbirds, that low-slung classy automobile.
Hers was white, with a removable black hardtop which had
chrome-lined portholes on each side and red leather interior
and a Continental kit on the trunk lid. Oh, it was beautiful,
Thunderbirds were certainly class automobiles. Getting into
it, she playfully raced the motor, then tossed her head and
flipped back her hair and waved gaily. "BYE," they said in
bunches of friendliness. "SEE YOU!"

And that, she thought, was that. Goodbye, girls, goodbye.
She'd done well.

Headed south in the direction of home, she pictured them
waiting for her . . . Carroll pacing before the picture window, his thumbs erect and twitching, waiting to study her
first step from the car to see if she stumbled or swayed, and
Preston busily not doing something he was pretending to
take an interest in, his eyes jumping with anxiety as he
stared down the road she should come down. Dear, dumb,
Preston, he tried so hard not to be obvious, he wanted so to
believe what he did was love her, that adoring was enough.
But—like the Jello pie family—they were only doing what
they had to, and that had run its course for her, had used it-

self up. And Serenthea . . . but she would not think of Serenthea. She could not afford to. Not again.

At the gravel road that led home, she gunned the motor until the speedometer hit ninety and stayed on the highway going west into the sun. The car took the speed easily and seemed to lower by several inches. It was a good feeling. Humming, the little black and white car raced on, headed toward Bryson's, in the direction of the river and across it, Arkansas.

You had to want either one so badly. Drinking carried such a price and the threat of sobriety an even higher one. No such thing as in-between. Drinking had been a way of easing out weeks, days, hours, minutes . . . those marks and dots and lines on clocks and calendars, those attempts at ordering time . . . into an unmeasured timeless oblivion which was *hers*. It had been a way, one she thought might not have been so much worse than some others, not as awful as they would have you believe, at any rate. And sober? Sober was, just as they called it, *dry*. Hopeless, lifeless, deathless, dreamless . . . if that was how it had to be, if drunkenness only led back again to enforced sobriety and dryness . . . little choice was left her that she could accommodate. She knew how it was now, being sober, and it was an accommodation she wasn't up to. You had to want either one very badly because the price of either was so high, and she knew of nothing satisfying in between. . . .

Opening the car window on her side, she turned the radio up high. She had made her decision so long ago, it was as if she had already carried it through. Now was only shadow play, the acting out, which was easy. She drove toward the bridge. The state line was in the middle of the river somewhere, another line, another lie, some other futile attempt at

measurement and control. None of it was real. At the toll
booth, she paid her fifty cents and chatted amiably with the
attendant, a warty old man whose radio also played loud
music, tuned to the same local station as hers. Neither having lowered the volume, they shouted over the radios, com-
plimenting one another on the weather as if each held the
other responsible. Yes, she said with gratitude, *wasn't* it a
lovely day! And so early for such days too . . . weren't the
days getting shorter? After five, and the sun was beginning
to set, and didn't they remember when it wasn't dark until
eight, not more than a week or so ago! She laughed with
him and gave him her company and was as accommodating
to his conversation and expectations as she had been the
women at the party. As she waved and drove off, he tipped
his hat and in her mirror she saw him sit back down in his
chair and tilt it back again, where he would stay until someone else came along with whom he could carry on the same
conversation all over again, more of the same, more of the
same, only perhaps with some slight difference, a request for
road directions, the need for change, a match, information
. . . essentially however the same and the same and then
the same again coming back at you endlessly.

Was monotony haunting her? Had she hit on it?

It was when she saw the Jello pie, little-note woman come
back to Bryson that she had decided. Six days after her
speech, her husband's arms heavy on her shoulders, so that
the woman seemed about to collapse under the weight, and
in her drink-heavy eyes such a tormented possessed look
. . . you had to want things so, you had to *want* to be
drunk, you had to *want* to live in a family, you had to want
not to. You had to need to escape it. And resort to the drinking again and again; it went on and on, boring, monotonous.

And once the woman's husband left, she had collapsed into the arms of her fellow dreamers, home again, starting the whole thing over as if it were new. You had to be very tied to a family to run from it so desperately. You had to hate them so much you believed you loved them. You had to want to love them . . . you had to want . . . that was when she had decided what to do.

The first part of the bridge was low, as it crossed over swamplike pools and ponds. Beneath it, you could see the tops of willow trees, but no water. "River rats" lived down there, in shanties and shacks and abandoned railroad cars and trailers, in tents and buses and what-have-you, scurrying like their namesakes for dry spots when the river rose and their piece of yard turned to slush and river bottom. No one bothered them there, the land belonged to no one, and sometimes was not land at all. Like rats, they went where shelter was. Sometimes, down through the whipping willow branches you could see bits and pieces of their wash—a glance of bright color, quick movement all white—flapping in the wind. But Lady did not look down. Ahead, the main part of the bridge loomed high, a silver mountain, glittering in the sun's last light, shining again in the water, shining in between in the air itself. Barges slid lazily under it. Because of the heavy spring rains, the river was still high, and though muddy, sparkling. The sun, resting on finger tips of the trees, was just beginning to turn bloody. When it was gone the water would be brown again. Lady gripped the wheel and kept her eyes ahead. She felt the steel ridges of the structure go by underneath, but the car took the unevenness well; she felt it only as a slight rumbling, no more. And then the rails on either side of her began to get higher, as she entered the girdered tunnel. This was the main part of the bridge, over the deepest part of the water where, somewhere, the state line was. Slowing, she looked out beyond the steel girders at the water. Like the tollhouse keeper, it made the same conversation day after day after day and yet, like him, never translated it as monotony, only as life itself, as it came and was. Well, she wished them luck. When she reached what seemed to her the very middle, the highest point, she stopped the car, shifted it to *park*, and cut the motor. The radio went off. All she could hear was the wind, whistling through cables and wires and pipes and beams. What a thing, she thought, was a bridge! To set your life on building something like that . . . that would be worth a person's time. That would fill you up and tell you what to do. She got out of the Thunderbird, taking her purse. The wind whipped her hair and slapped strings into her eyes and flattened the ruffles of her blouse in one direction. Pulling a handkerchief out of her purse, she held it up and let the wind take it. At first it stayed in front of her, motionless there. It seemed not to want to fly at all and she thought it would come directly back to her. Then a gust picked it up and twirled it, lifting it over her head and far out over the water . . . it was gone, floating, graceful. Through sunglasses, Lady watched as it drifted at the wind's whim and stayed in the air for a long time before finally, its downward course suddenly overtaking its yen to fly, it disappeared beneath the bridge.

A car approached from the opposite direction, going back to Eunola. Lady hurried around the front of the Thunderbird to the sidewalk that ran the length of the bridge and, turning around, leaned back on a pipe of the railing there, facing her car. The other car passed, slowed down, then began backing up. Lady slipped out of her sling-pump navy shoes and dropped her purse beside her shoes.

The bridge was made of such stunningly bright silver: it looked like a child's toy, apt to break, or some fantasy gown of silver lamé . . . something fragile; she wondered if it would bend with the weight of her and collapse when she stood on it. The man was out of his car now, waving and yelling, struggling to get across the barrier that ran between lines of traffic and separated him from her. Lady reached above her head for two steel struts to grab hold of and, her back still to the river, hoisted herself up onto the pipe. Placing her feet, she noticed her shoes. They were just as she had stepped out of them: toes turned primly in toward one another. After all those lessons, she still walked pigeon-toed! Well . . . she would have her small vices in spite of them all. Later, the man struggling to get to her from the other side of the barrier remembered that she smiled when she looked up, as if to reassure him she was happy with what she was doing. That smile was passed on, to become a permanent part of the story told of her for years to come, as well as the sweet happy conversation with the tollhouse keeper and the high-spirited bridge game. No one knew it was her shoes and the irony there and her love for that, the slightly ludicrous remark, the gently sarcastic gesture, the unserious eye, that gave her a lift and made her smile.

Lady didn't think any more then. All the preparations and decisions having been made, there was only the execution left, the simplest part. She held on to the steel struts with her arms out, spread out leaning backward, her body swinging free in the middle, as certain of what she was doing and what she was giving up and what she did not want badly enough to endure tedium and live sober for as the man who was trying to get to her: he meant to save her. But it was long over. She simply closed her eyes and let go. Went backward so she couldn't see it come to her or her to it but would fall free of its ending. The man, panicked, screamed as she went, and still fought to reach her even though she was gone. Nothing was there when he finally got across but her shoes and purse and, of course, the car. He looked in her purse to find out who she was, but she had taken out her wallet beforehand and left no clue and so the highway patrol had to trace the car. It was well dark by the time they contacted Preston and drove the car out to him. He told them to put the car in the garage, shut the door behind it and leave it there. They found no note; she had said no farewells. As far as they knew, it was hers. All hers.

From that height Lady's body hit the water as if it were concrete, but her mind took no note of it and she felt no pain, except in her imagination, which reeled as she dropped, letting her know how it would be. She kept throwing her arms behind her . . . like a panicky baby trying to catch itself and keep from falling . . . something in her looking for the base, a ground, something to latch on to, to cushion the blow. The last thing she was aware of was a familiar notion of impatience, that intolerable tingling in her belly that meant things were not going fast enough . . . dear God would it never be over, would even this take so long, could she not enjoy what she had so desperately sought . . . and a kind of wonder that falling took so long, that she actually had time to think, and feel so angry.

The funeral was well attended. Preston bowed his bald head and struggled with what he knew, trying to compre-

hend what she had done and accommodate it into his life.
But it would not fit. He didn't know what to do with it. He
said nothing to well-wishers but only smiled nervously, his
mouth fidgeting as if attached to rubber bands. Sweat
popped out on his flushed bald head; he kept wiping it
away. Next to him, Carroll stood rigidly, not bowing his
head even when the service called for it. Furious, defeated,
having received his mother's angry message quite clearly
. . . he sulked. The corners of his mouth turned down in a
characteristic scowl. Some Garden Club and bridge party ladies came, as did several cotton men. Lady's mother, who
had shriveled until she was only a bare white wisp, fragile
and constantly doped, like a tattered lace handkerchief spotted with old perfume, teetered above the grave and held on
to her black picture hat and seemed about to fall in herself.
Beside her, Lady's father stood slumped and wheezing, a
man so disillusioned by bad turns that one more indication of
life's disorder hardly fazed him. Mattie Sue and Jewel, an-
cient Cunninghams, so old and unused to getting out that
they creaked in the weather, had unwrapped their moth-
balled blacks for the funeral and were also there. Mattie Sue
muttered the whole time, reiterating her unflagging disgust
with the male sex in general, including the chauffeur, the
preacher, and the boy acolytes assisting. It was men, she
believed, who had taken away what rightfully belonged to
her—her own heritage, passed on by Sexton, not to Samuel
but to *her*—and she was certain if men didn't cause Lady's
death they at least played a big part in her reasons. Jewel
. . . Bit . . . was barely present. Her attention, like a thistle
blowing this way and that in the wind, kept from leaving altogether only by the tiniest silk-thin thread . . . scattered. It
traveled with noise and movement, shifting this way, sliding

there, as she turned to look at birds, coughs, airplanes, a squirrel, a car, her head pivoting about, until Mattie Sue put a firm arm around her shoulder to keep her from wandering more.

Serenthea came when the service was over and everyone was gone, to mourn Lady's death in her own way. There had been one note sent, after all, left beneath her pillow where Serenthea would be certain to find it. "Serenthea," it said, "the only one, the only one. Let this help you. LB Cunningham." Enclosed were ten five-hundred-dollar bills which Serenthea accepted more as a gift of her grace than as means to her own comfort. She buried the bills inside her mattress, and valuing them too much to spend, never used them.

Serenthea longed for Lady and grieved for her. She *felt* the absence of her, as real and palpable as her presence had been, and continued to feel it for the rest of her life. The longing never lessened in intensity; she never missed her less strongly or stopped wishing she were alive; time did no healing. She sang to Lady and wept over her . . . her grave was next to Samuel's, who lay beside Graham, the only Cunninghams since Sexton to die . . . and apologized to her all her life. She told Judge: "Death was on her that day and I saw it. It was like a crown on her head. The way she talked and told me her heartfelt tales before she went, how she gave me her reasons and desires and the way she told me goodbye and kept on telling me goodbye, goodbye, Serenthea, she kept on saying, goodbye, goodbye. Lord, I knew something, I did, and I tried to get her not to go . . . but, oh, there is nothing I would not give to go back now and *keep* her from going. Death lay on her head that day. I wish I had listened to my heart and kept her from going." The ground covering Lady's grave was never still but stayed constantly stirred by Serenthea's visiting and raking and planting and clearing and replanting, with the seasons, and by her reaching down into it with her grief and such wails and moans and keenings it seemed she might even brighten her back to life they were so powerful and had such thrust. She went every day until the day she, Serenthea, died too.

XI

SEXTON

Dust unto dust,
To this all must;
The tenant hath resign'd
The faded form
To waste and worm—
Corruption claims her kind.

Through paths unknown
Thy soul hath flown,
To seek the realms of woe.
Where fiery pain
Shall purge the stain
Of actions done below.

In that sad place,
By Mary's grace,
Brief may thy dwelling be!

Till prayers and alms
And holy psalms
Shall set the captive free.

Purgatory.

Sexton never knew. He hadn't read the book or the poem.
All he knew was it was from *Ivanhoe,* which was about a
brave and daring knight.

XII

HOMECOMING

Carroll was in the stands Homecoming night when Lolly came home to twirl, and so was Booth Oates—standing by the fence in Frank's old place while Frank waited in the car. Lucille was home, in bed, her eyes so dry and pushed open from what she had seen that she thought she might never sleep again. And James Blue was gone, having been transferred a month before to an air force base somewhere in Greenland, a place called Thule. Lolly wore her Eunola gold-spangled uniform and when she marched on to the field, someone raised a sign saying "WELCOME HOME, LOLLY . . . EUNOLA'S OWN!" The Homecoming Court was circling the field as Lolly strutted into the end zone and stayed a little too long, past her usual time. The girls were primping and blinking mascaraed eyes and smiling. Last year's nobody, Faye Spivey of all people, was this year's queen. Faye was a Peavey, Zhena's daughter. She was five-foot-nine, and played last-chair French horn in the band;

she had size-nine feet, drab, dirt-colored hair, big ankles and acne. But it was an unwritten tradition at EHS to elect as Homecoming Queen an unknown girl, who went steady with (and, even more emphatically unwritten, put out for) a football player; in Faye's case, a shy uncelebrated left end. Girls who had been Homecoming maids every year before their senior year were still Homecoming maids their last time out, because nobody moved up to queen. Queen came from nowhere. But in Faye's case it did seem the tradition was being taken a little too literally. She was perhaps from a bit too far out in nowhere for comfort. Maids pouted, mothers complained as they stitched up long dresses, but there wasn't a thing they could do about it, tradition was tradition. Faye was hunched over in her convertible trying to look short, holding her chrysanthemums so tight the leaves bruised. Her face was covered with Ac-no-mel and her lips trembled from staying so long in a smile. Zhena, of course, was in the stands too, and Lee Spivey her husband, and all the other Eunola Peaveys except Lucille. On her way, batting feet out of her path, was Granny, headed for a seat. She had said she would like to see Faye crowned, but refused to come for the game, and so Esker had gone out and gotten her just before halftime, and here she came. She didn't tell them she came as much to see Lolly as Faye. Furious as ever, she entered, glaring. "Lord," said Zhena under her breath, "she's wearing her hat." And Lee turned to see. "Esker," Zhena whispered, "why'd you let her wear that *hat?*" But Esker just shrugged, he wasn't about to tell her to take a hat off, not him; all they told him was to get her and he did, nothing was said about hats. It had been Matthew's church hat, which she turned into a planting one. It used to be cream-colored with a sporty black silk band around the crown, but by now a dog had pulled off the band and she had sweated through the cream color as well as several dogs having peed on it, and turned it into a sickly kind of color, like coffee that's sat for a day or so with milk in it. Granny jammed the hat square down on her head, not turned to the side at a jaunty angle the way Matthew wore it but square down hard, a serious no-nonsense, get-in-the-ground-you-fucking-petunia-seed hat. The snap in the brim remained, but now peaked right down between her eyes, exactly in the middle of them at the bridge of her nose, which made Granny look more than slightly cross-eyed, with her tiny eyes bunched together like a vise closing in on the brim's snap.

Sucking her gums, she grunted and sat down.

Her dress was of a stretched-out jersey which sagged at the sides and drew up in the middle. Across the neck of the dress, holding it together where a button was missing, was a brooch she jealously protected and rarely wore. It had belonged to her mother and maybe *her* mother as well, and Granny had vowed no daughter of hers would get it. It was a beautiful piece, the hand-painted bust of a woman, set against an ivory-colored oval. The woman's hair was piled loosely on her head, with soft curls dangling around her face and neck. Her eyes were soft and warm, her skin pearly, her lips pink and promising. Above and below this brooch the worn dirty dress gaped open and revealed her peach-colored camisole. She wore Matthew's old maroon wool cardigan, and had rolled her hose high enough that when she walked you couldn't see her garters but when she sat down you could.

Granny created quite a stir at the Homecoming game. As she walked, rolling side to side, knocking people to the right

and left with Matthew's solid oak cane, her body large and
hefty, her head so small it seemed shrunken, a walnut head,
and cursed and muttered hoarsely under her breath, everyone turned to look. They'd never seen anything to beat it at
a football game in Eunola, not in the good seats. Johnnie
Ruth had bought her some men's tennis shoes to wear
around the house and do her planting in, low quarter black
basketball-type shoes, and she had them on now, with the
laces open and the ends straggling about her feet. Not in the
good seats, never before.

She sat on the front row with her legs wide apart, the
cane between, one hand on it and one on a knee, with both
elbows cocked out to give her plenty of room. In a small
sack in her sweater pocket was her baking powder can, half-
full.

As Lolly neared the fifty-yard line, the majorettes, all
thumbs, fumed as they twirled, unhappy that last year's star
was monopolizing their show, and the crowd screamed her
name. Granny turned around and looked up into the stands,
growling. Such fools. Several rows back, a cocky young
blond-headed boy caught her eye. There was such an arro-
gant tilt to his head and such a sly unsteadied nonchalance
about his gray-green eyes that Granny knew right away who
he was. She'd heard he was home but Preston hadn't been
by in a while, since Lady's event, and she knew little about
the boy. Laughing, he passed a silver flask behind him and
with a large, ironed white handkerchief wiped his mouth.
He was drunk . . . which figured . . . but when he looked
down and caught Granny's eyes she saw the lifelessness
there—having nothing to do with alcohol—sparked only by a
sharp gleam of intelligence. A leveled-out plane was in his
head. A fixedness like hers. He was not a part of this

foolishness and never would be, not any of Eunola's foolishness. No more than she had been. He was Lady's boy all
right.

Then his eyes lifted and he pointed to the field where
Lolly was and stood and said something that made others
around him stand too. And the standing and remarking
moved down, passed, from Carroll to both sides of him and
behind and in front of, one to the other. Something had happened which he was the first to see. Granny turned to find
out what had caused the commotion.

Lolly had kept all the provisions her benefactors had set
down. But there was another one they hadn't thought of,
which it wouldn't have helped if they had because it had already happened when they made up the contract. Had Vale
Batson not been quite so discreet he would have caught it
. . . had he had the nerve to check her "females." Word
spread quickly, and those who didn't want to see at first did,
quickly enough, like the people with magnifying glasses in-
specting the YPC camp brochures, they came up from their
huddled examination joined together in anger and outrage.
Most stood, and beating their fists in the air, booed. And
Lolly, who hadn't decided what she was going to do yet but
was hoping to slide through this one occasion and make her
mind up afterward, saw the truth dawn on them in ripples,
but, knowing little else to do for the time being, kept twirling and marching, watching for signs of violence. She was a
girl not meant to understand tragedy, she thought practice
and wanting a thing bad enough would do, in a case like
this or any other, without fear or love just doing what you
had to. And the depth of her feelings at that moment went
no farther than when she failed at a twirling maneuver. It
was simply turning out differently from what she had ex-

pected, that was all, and she would have to find new plans.

When they threw the sign down on the field and seemed to be lifting up out of the stands in a collective heave, Lolly executed a sharp left turn and headed off the field.

The court kept circling and Faye Spivey smiled away, as if all the commotion was for her.

Booth was jumping up and down and clapping his hands and yelling "Lah-LEE! Lah-LEE!" and Granny sat leaning on the crook of her cane, smiling. The people were outraged. She had duped them, thrown them over, violated their trust, corrupted their dream, vulgarized their astonishment. She was, as if to spite them after all their denials, a trailer tramp . . . at heart a Peavey. Granny was delighted. "'At away," she muttered to herself, sucking her gums with relish. "You show 'em, girl, you go ahead and do it. Git 'em!" And Lolly marched on off the field, in a high controlled strut, her chin up, the tip of it high in the air like the point of a valentine guiding her. The band was still playing and Faye was still smiling and Granny deep under her hat was grinning, while the other Peaveys sat stone-faced, furious and outraged. Bo's face turned a bright scarlet and his mouth drew down into a quivering smirk. Johnnie Ruth and Zhena exchanged hot looks: Lucille had never had anything to do with any of the rest of them, had never contributed one thing they could count on except trouble, and now that Faye had something going for her, her and Frank's high and mighty offspring had to ruin it . . . Frank, who never gave anybody the time of day, especially Peaveys.

Hearing the uproar, certain of its cause, he ran from the car, through the parking lot, to the field to get her. He would not have her hurt. She was coming off the field.

Booth met her first. He had been so confused. His family

had had to resort to locking him in the house on Sundays to
keep him from bicycling out to the trailer house to see her
. . . for no matter how many times he went and found her
gone he would continue to go, Sunday after Sunday, not
knowing why or understanding that if something happened
a number of times it was likely to happen again, just going.
Pure and simple: Sundays . . . going. Now he was happy
again. He was seeing her. When she got to the gate, he
offered his hand and reached for her but she didn't look in
his direction; she ran for Frank, who covered her with a
sweater and hurried away with her.

After Faye was crowned—and Granny thought she looked
perfectly ridiculous with that rhinestone tiara sitting high
up on her tightly-curled hair—Pauline, oldest child and most
severely religious of Granny's eight and therefore the most
outraged, said she and her husband would take Granny
home as they did not care to see the rest of the game.
Granny didn't say a word the whole way except to grunt
and complain and let Pauline's husband know she disap-
proved of him and everything he did including how he
drove a car. When they let her out, Granny went and sat
in her rocking chair and laughed out loud. The dogs even
perked up their ears, it was such a different sound from her
usual angry bellows. She stomped her foot and pounded her
cane against the porch floor and rocked herself back and
forth and back and forth, laughing so loud the owls in Sexton's oak could hear it and the rats out there woke up.
Laughed and laughed. Every time she thought about those
idiots standing up so puny and stark-raving crazy mad, she
laughed again. It fit . . . it fit . . . she loved it.

Her laughter pealed over the rotting cotton stalks surrounding her house, the very ones James and Lolly had

watched sprout and bloom, which in Lolly's absence had been picked clean, except for leftover shreds and wisps of white and the brown curling leaves and stems.

It was a night to remember, and Eunola didn't get over it for a long time. They were to talk about it in years to come as *the* night. "Seemed like something sort of ended that night," they would say. After the game, Carroll, full drunk by then, untouched by the scandal of Lolly's pregnancy, raced to Sunflower, competing against nobody but himself and time, the Roadmaster against itself. Homecoming was meaningless to him, and as he didn't have a date with a high school girl he couldn't get into the dance and would have been bored anyway, and so he got into the Roadmaster and went to the stoplight and put his foot down and raced anyway. He was alone and drunk and had no place else to go. The Roadmaster had lost its allure for the others by then, as they became too used to its success and Carroll's patronage and were looking for other things to run until it or they gave out. The Roadmaster moved on past the Dairy Delite, slowly picking up speed, past thirty, thirty-two, thirty-three, thirty-four, mile by mile, the red pointed streak moving steadily across the dash, a mile marker at a time.

It was a hot night for late October. Clouds hung low and ran by fast beneath the stars. The highway was wide open ahead of him with very little traffic going either way. The road was his and all he had, from stoplight to stoplight, Gold 'n' Crust to Sunflower, and nobody to be with at either end. Preston had said if he didn't do something, one thing or another and soon, the Army was going to get him, but Carroll knew better, the draft never got a Beall that didn't want to go. He thought of Lady. How she had drifted, what she had done. He resented it. It was a message aimed directly at him. He had intended to get to her. He had meant to find out. But not to have it go so far. She had cheated. "Call me Lady." *Lady.* The radio was on full blast and Carroll's flask of bourbon lay on the seat next to him. Up to seventy now, he passed a Greyhound bus with all the lights on inside, filled with people milling about, obviously partying. When he got ahead of it, Carroll looked in the mirror to see where it was headed but the sign over the windshield said only "CHARTERED." Carroll could see the driver's face, blank and concentrating, removed from the gaiety around him. The bus was going fast—for a bus—sixty-five or so.

She had taken it with her. Rather than give him the least hint of it, had taken it and thrown it from a bridge, as easily as she might toss away a discarded tissue. And smiling, the one witness said: smiling. How much time she must have spent planning it. Honing her weapon, sharpening it, smiling as she pictured his reaction. "Bitch," he said aloud, and pressed his palm to the left side of his chest to ease the aching there. He supposed it was his heart; sometimes it hurt, without warning or cause. Sometimes if he lay too long on that side he woke up in the night feeling it squeezed and mashed inside his chest, and it hurt so to move that he had to take a great deal of time turning over. It might take as long as five minutes to get from his left side onto his back. Tears came from somewhere; his vision blurred. He returned his hand to the wheel. The red streak reached eighty, and the chartered bus receded in his rearview mirror. So beautiful and sure, maintaining her body. And for what? To stay on a shelf like Serenthea's peaches, in sterilized, waxed, and tight-lidded jars?

When he drove past the trailer park, up to one-fifteen, if

Carroll had looked, or known where to, he would have seen
all the lights on in the Lasswell trailer. Zhena Spivey, Lucille's sister, was overseeing the packing of Lolly's clothes,
and the girl's departure. She was going to Tennessee, where
Ola Faye now lived. Ola Faye was a middle Peavey, one
down from Zhena, and Zhena said Lolly had to leave right
away and not come back to Eunola, ever. Frank sat outside,
smoking, watching the clouds, taking no part in the pro-
ceedings. The situation had gone too far beyond what he
understood, and he let them do what they thought best because pregnancy, like religion, death, and sickness, was a
woman's concern he felt ignorant to deal with. He looked
ahead, holding on to what he had left of the Frank Lasswell
he had once spoken of with some pride. It was all he had
now, and he fixed hard on it. Absorbed in this, he heard Carroll's car move by fast . . . something barely taken notice of
. . . but paid little attention. Lolly watched them pack, saying nothing, only waiting for them to finish. Waiting to feel
something. She knew she should and wanted to, but nothing
came. And with Lucille and Zhena tearing around so, and
Frank so pent up and silent, there seemed little left for her
to feel; they had taken it all on for her, were speaking in her
place. And so she let them go ahead, and waited for something else to come to her. Surely it would happen soon, and
she would be overcome with grief or unhappiness or shame
. . . something . . . if no one else took it from her before
she had a chance to know what it was. Lucille, to everyone's surprise, came out of her room and helped pack, in
fact did so with such intensity Zhena finally had to tell her
to slow down, they didn't have to catch a plane or anything.

Just past the trailer camp, across the highway on Carroll's
left, was a large clump of trees, mostly pines, growing tight

together, so that you could hardly see through them at all, and just past the trees was a cotton field. Two hundred acres, all of it in bloom now, ready for harvesting. Rains had come just at the right time the summer before to encourage plants to sprout and make squares, and the autumn sun had been more gentle and less drying than usual, so the field was lush with yield now. It would be a good year, cotton planters were saying, if only the market held. Tall full plants went on and on, until they seemed to merge; green full bodies, with soft white moonish heads.

Coming out of the clump of trees, Carroll looked in that direction and felt a sudden panic. The trees had made a firm boundary, a kind of tunnel . . . now there was only openness, space; he panicked. As a low, gray smoky cloud drifted past it, he could see the moon, low in the sky. And under it, space. Too much room for falling. Suddenly, he took his foot from the accelerator, drew both legs up against the seat, held on to the steering wheel until his knuckles were white. But he couldn't keep his eyes off the horizon. And the space.

He thought he felt what she had. That falling, unsupported, beyond trust and help and old assumptions, hands grabbing desperately behind for an edge, the bottom, a cushion. Too much space. With only the imagination to say what was next, and the mind trying to black that out, trying to negate anticipation and give in to the falling. The falling. It cut through the threads binding his heart and flooded through him. The pain in his side lifted and a rush—something warm—came up from there, and filled his mind. Startled, Carroll, still gripping the steering wheel, turned in that direction, toward the openness, and the Buick veered sharply, its tires screeching on the pavement in a terrible, resisting wail.

Something said *hold on* while another voice told him *let go*. The Buick went across the two left-hand lanes—there was no traffic—jumped the small ditch beside the highway, actually flew over it, and then . . . his feet still flat against the seat, he was not pressing the Roadmaster on, it was going on its own momentum . . . and something again said *hold on* while another voice refuted that, and chanted *let go, let go*. He blacked out.

Frank heard it—there was a screaming and then a terrible, deep thud—but he did not even turn his head. Inside, Lucille looked up from the packing and said, "What was that?" but Zhena, busy talking, hadn't heard, and so they went back to their work, though Lucille's impeccable senses told her there had been an accident of some kind. Lolly, too, knew it was something terrible. An inhuman sound like that. It was like bones rolled up in a dream, crashing into your night. She covered her ears.

If the earth hadn't been so soft, the car might not have slowed down so mercifully. It might have kept on and on. As fast as it had been going, it might have run all the way through the cotton field to the ditch on the other side or into the pine trees to the south. Instead, after flying across the small ditch, the Roadmaster plowed into the earth some twenty yards past it and all but came to a stop there. Its tires in black gumbo up past their midsections, the car was forced to leave some of its momentum in that downward plunge, and by the time it started going on its way again, its forward thrust had been blunted, reined, brought to a halt by the sucking force of the deep wet fertile earth. And so, after struggling a pitiful fifty feet or so more, the Roadmaster, as if in a childish fit of temper, turned sharply to its right and then very gently and agilely, in one uncomplicated and very beautiful gesture, turned over on that side, the right, and stayed, its two left-hand tires spinning in the air.

Let go! the voice urged, his heart pounding so hard and free it seemed about to break his chest in two. *Let go!*

The driver of the chartered bus pulled over and stopped, and its passengers poured out to come across the highway and be the first to see. Although their feet sank in the soft black dirt of the rowed-up field and they trampled down the perfectly good cotton already in bloom there, they came on undeterred, with topsoil and cotton inside their shoes, looking on the ground as they went, hoping to find the driver had been thrown out into the soft ground instead of staying inside the Buick.

Frank loaded Lolly's suitcase into the trunk of the car, slammed down the lid, and got in to wait for her. Through the picture window, he could see Lucille inside the trailer. She looked like a crippled, half-crazed bird trying to fly with one wing. Back and forth she went, her head jerking about, her eyes popping from her head, her mouth tight and pulled. Her forehead was broad and high—still smooth and milky white, flawless, without a wrinkle. She moved with such energy, such intensity . . . God, before all this and after, now that so much had gone by and was lost . . . still, the love of his life. Her eyes were clear and bright, filled with expectancy. His one acknowledgment of the presence of hope in the world, his ever-so-slight return greeting to the nod of possibility.

Zhena came and led her to bed.

When they managed to tip the car back over onto all four wheels, they discovered Carroll was not in it. By then, someone had brought a high-beam flashlight, and they trained it in the direction the car had come from to find him. But he was not that far; he was right beside the Roadmaster, curled up on his side in the dirt by the edge of the passenger door.

Before the car turned on its side, he had let go of the steering wheel; released, the wheel had gone crazily back and forth, then, propelled by a slight rise in the earth, had turned sharply right. When the Roadmaster rolled on its side, Carroll had tumbled across the seat, and when it was steadily upended there, had become wedged in the open window on that side. So that when they turned the car over, he had stayed exactly as he had landed; the window went back over, and he stayed. Curled up between cotton rows in a tight ball. Unconscious, he looked like a baby there, like something so pitifully small it might be scooped up with one hand and carried off. One arm was thrown over his face, that wrist unnaturally cocked, and there was a tear across that cheek. Otherwise, his body seemed unharmed, at least what they could see of it, lying there. Fearful of complicating any internal injuries he might have sustained, they left him there until help arrived. In a circle around him, they stood looking down, until somebody came who knew who he was, when they began gently calling his name. "Carroll . . . ? Carroll . . . ?"

As Frank and Lolly drove north on 84, ambulances and fire trucks and wreckers screamed past, cocooned in blinking lights, red and yellow-white, colors carrying sound, all blurred together, speed, sound, light, urgency.

"I knew something terrible happened," Lolly whispered.

When they passed the scene of the accident, lights were trained on the field, beating paths up and down it, and cars were parked all along the highway. In the headlights of the trucks and cars and the searchlight of the wrecker, they could see people standing in a circle looking down, beside a car.

"My God . . ."

"It's the Roadmaster."

The car was lit up center stage, the mint green on one side as wrinkled as a tissue, the dark green hardtop unscratched. Its four chrome-encircled exhaust holes and the two chrome strips across the trunk picked up the light and sparkled, announcing to the world this still was what it had always been, the biggest, heaviest thing going, IT, the car, the Roadmaster. Looking as majestic and imperturbable as ever. And next to it, Carroll's body, like a piece of soft fruit on the earth.

After slowing down somewhat, Frank went back to his usual careful traveling rate, went on north, neither of them saying much. Behind him, he heard the ambulance, screaming its way back to Eunola. Before they crossed the state line, Lolly was asleep, curled on the seat beside him as warm and safe inside herself as a cat.

XIII

THE DREAM

BOOTH

Eunola police got another call Homecoming night. From Rose Leuckenbach. Rose's garage apartment was located not far from where Booth Oates lived, and she called to say he had been peering in her window.

"I was undressing," she said calmly to two policemen on her front porch, "when I heard something on the stairs, and when I looked over I could see him, and of course I recognized his voice. He was saying something." Rose stood resolutely against her door, reviewing facts as facilely as she measured and removed inches. "I tried to shoo him away. I said 'Go home, Booth Oates!' But he started howling and screaming and crying and beating on the window. That's when I decided I could not restrain him alone and called you. Then, as if he knew, he clattered down the stairs and I heard him fooling with my bicycle and came out and saw him down there at the foot of the stairs. You see? Three spokes. Kicked out. He ran off, still screaming something, the same thing he was screaming at my window, I don't know what, then he was gone . . . on *his* bicycle. He rides one too, you know. Officer, the man was berserk. This kind of behavior cannot go unchecked and that is all there is to it."

Rose's hair was loose and hung to her waist, bent at the nape of her neck where an elastic ordinarily held it. She wore a man's flannel robe with a dark tasseled sash around her waist. When she finally finished—it was quite a harangue —Rose informed the policemen she was going to bed, and when one asked if he might use her telephone first she flatly refused and turned and went into her apartment, slamming the door square in their faces, locking it behind her.

They found Booth pedaling out the highway in the direction of the crash. He didn't seem berserk any more, though there were streams of dirt running down his face, where he had been crying. He was calmer now, intent on getting where he was going. All he said when they stopped him was "Lah-Lee. Lah-LEE. Lah-LEE." Over and over again. They tried to be gentle with him and get him to go with them voluntarily, but every time somebody looked the other way or let go of him, Booth bolted, his mind fixed on one thing only: her. Finally they had to handcuff him and toss him in the back seat. They strapped his bicycle to the trunk. All the way back into town he cried for her. "Lah-LEE . . ."

The Oateses, chagrined by the notoriety and suspicion of violence, took Booth away the next day. They drove him to a state institution where people said he could pine away and dream about his Lah-LEE forever. But Booth never did that, because unless he had something familiar to remind him or a routine to go by, his memory extended no farther than the pinprick of a lost second, and so, without Sundays going to her or Saturdays waxing his bike, he lost her altogether and lived in that place in one room in an endlessly recurring present. At the mercy of each appearing moment, outside all sequence and patterns and accumulations . . . one . . . one . . . making no more connections at all.

EUNOLA

It was then that Lolly's legend and Booth's and the Roadmaster's were magnified. People reminisced, and embroidered stories about them and with the three of them absent, their adventures became so exaggerated no one who was there would have recognized them as the same ones they had seen. Just as people had done when Graham died, they kept remembering, and, as in the case of Lady's smile, kept changing the remembering.

Remember when . . . remember the time she . . . did you see Booth when he . . . when the Roadmaster took . . . when she had *two*, both on fire, and then . . . as if it had happened years before, and they were as long buried as Sexton in his old used-up cemetery.

Things quieted down a bit after all that, in the way events seem to come rhythmically to a boil, then settle back and laze out for a while. The highway patrol stationed a squad car between Eunola and Sunflower to stop the kids from running the ten-miler, which didn't keep them from revving up their cars for scratch-off contests and quarter-mile runs on the gravel and blacktop roads out toward Granny Pea-

vey's house. There was an accident out that way which mu-
tilated two boys hungry for cheese, leaving one with an am-
putated leg and the other with a broken neck and a head so
shaken apart that before his mother could reteach him the
alphabet she had to go back to first learnings and teach him
what words and reading were for. But other than that . . .
and the EHS Hornets winning the Big Eight Conference
and the unease when a certain decision was handed down
by the Supreme Court, and the state suddenly after all these
years deciding to legalize Eunola's longest-established custom, the buying and drinking of liquor together, and the
very controversial arrival of a rug factory nearby . . . the
town was pretty quiet for a while.

Rose pedaled away as usual, hitching up bosoms, sub-
tracting would-be candidates from the tax rolls before they
ever drew breath.

And Alberta gave to the cause.

And Carroll woke up, two days after the accident, surprised to find he had done it, himself wondering at himself,
that he had listened to one voice over the other. There was a
cast on one leg, and one on an arm, and some scratches, and
a pain deep in his diaphragm, but his head felt light and
clear and his breathing came easy. Preston was beside his
bed, staring at him. He would not, in fact, take his eyes off
the boy.

And Lolly waited, and held on to her very clear and distinct memories of twirling and the parades and games, but
lost the silver stream which, like a morning's attempt at re-

call of a dream, kept fading and drifting. Like a drop of mercury spilled from a broken thermometer, it kept slipping away. However she concentrated, however slowly and carefully she pressed her finger down and tried to capture it, it escaped.

Still . . . if she could just keep the focus outside herself. Concentrate. If she didn't feel what she didn't want to and refused to let the others bog her down, she just might be able to salvage some of the dream, eventually. Not all, certainly, but enough to get her out of the predicament she was in so that she could create her own drifts and endings, instead of it going on the way it was now, plotted out in advance.

She held on, giving nothing not directly asked for, even to the life growing inside her.

PRESTON

Attuned to the long run, he watched over Carroll and saw that he was taken care of and healed properly. And worked. So that he wouldn't think of Lady. Set himself down and put his attention on what needed him, the land around him. Dogged in keeping on as custom had taught him to, doing it steadily if with lessened interest now. Thinking of the boy . . . there had to be something . . . keeping on; doing it; working. Habit carried him; for that he was grateful. And whatever Carroll wanted, Preston saw that he had. After the boy came home, he watched over him like a patient mother cat, nursing his wounds, taking him wherever he wanted to go until he could get there on his own. It was at his son's suggestion that he began to sell some of the land Sexton had accumulated. He had need for less now, and the boy had been studying charts and market reports, and seemed to know.

CARROLL

He wheeled himself from room to room, and sat long hours at the window, watching as the cotton was harvested and the ground left to lie for another winter. He ordered books, watched market fluctuations, read about the nature of the land he lived on. And he began to envision a direction he could take; how his life might go. When he could walk again, he went to the gin office, studied the books there, watched how it was operated, made suggestions, and little by little began to take over the running of the Cunningham estate. When advance representatives of new industries came to Eunola, it was Carroll they went to talk to. And Carroll they found, of all the landowners there, by far the most amenable and willing to move on from old ideas and beliefs.

MATTIE SUE

The old woman banged her hand on a glass-topped table, rattling the silver tray, flipping over a spoon. So close! If Carroll had died, there would have been only the two of them left, she and Preston. Cursing, she stood up from the table, stared out the back window. There must be another way. She could not give up now. Not after coming so close. She'd get it yet. Her fair share. She'd get it yet.

FRANK

After letting her out at Ola Faye's, Frank refused to spend the night but only kissed Lolly briefly, held her close, and left her there . . . crying slightly, only, he suspected, because she was angry at being so out of control of her life. He went on. Got in his car and instead of going back south to Eunola, headed west. He crossed the river on the next bridge north from Eunola's, passed through one state, entered another, watching as he went the nature of the land around him as it changed: from—close to the river—green and wet and fertile, to—farther from it—rolling hills, to rockier plateaus, then drier flatlands. When he got so far from it that the very availability of water itself was crucial, he stopped. It was a dry and dusty place, where people lived in a temporary stance, expecting any day to be moved on, where the earth was packed and dry and gave little sustenance. Where, like the small trees growing there—which provided little shade or comfort or nourishment—people developed thin, light roots and sent them running out through the ground instead of down into it, because the earth there was unsuited for deep roots and therefore could not support a large shade or fruit tree.

He had left a family once before and not gone back; it was not so hard to do the second time. Having used up the terms of his contract in Eunola, it was best he went . . . his life was ground out. He went where there were fewer possibilities and almost no opening for hope anywhere. It suited him.

It was a place where people did not value the land. Where a man became quickly thin and set and worn. Where light-traveling people came to retire. A place for bones picked clean of meat. A graveyard, where hope was buried and each inhabitant its marker, a testament to its short life and long drawn-out death.

He worked for a pipeline company for a while and then on a highway construction crew, whatever he could get, moving up and down the state as jobs came and went, never settling or letting himself stay in one place long enough to feel comfortable or to come to recognize the signs and signals that the place or its weather gave out. He sent a letter to Lucille. He had wanted to say something about how he felt and why he was going and how heavy his heart felt and how full of disappointment and loneliness and caring for her. But the pen stayed over the paper not co-operating and all he said was: "Dear Lucille, I think it's best if I move on. Here's how much $$ we have in the bank. Buy yourself a

house if you want, it ought to be enough for down payment.
I'll send money every month. You can mail some on to her.
Also will keep up insurance payments so if anything hap-
pens to me you'll be okay. I wish it would have turned out
better. Frank."

He sent a generous amount every month; otherwise he
tried not to think of them. And so his life began to close in
and his vision to narrow . . . more and more until as time
went on he finally had it down to where he could manage it.
The scope of his life finally closed before him and all that
was left was a small crack, through which he could see but
one thing, its working out, all the way, until some ending
finally let him go.

LUCILLE

Lucille picked up an old piece of cloth one day, something
Lolly had left, and cut it out and began to piece it together
. . . something for the baby . . .

With so much gone, she had been able to find order in
what was left. Colors didn't run into one another now but
stood out, so that she could pick one and, undistracted, go
with it. One day, walking outside, she had noticed the sign
beside the trailer steps: "Lucille Lasswell, Sewing" . . . still
there, after all that time . . . and had pulled it up and put it
out for trash. Surprised no one had done it before . . . she
hadn't noticed it there . . .

I wish it would have turned out better.

What had happened? And could she pinpoint when?

They had been so hopeful. She with her good grades, he tearing tickets from a book to buy furniture in installments, the maple table, the platform rocker . . . now all that was left was that puny wish. And the generous amounts of money he sent. Now she took her life in small spoonfuls, swallowing what came bit by bit, without fretting about the one after. Or how it would taste. Holding very still in bright unearthly calm, as in the eye of a hurricane when the earth itself seems to stand still and the air takes on an unnaturally golden glow and people feel at the same time blessed and damned, as if they'd suddenly been taken off the earth and put at the heart of its deepest mysteries . . . she sat making clothes for Lolly's baby. Her head was very still and very bright; she knew winds of the old madness whirled about her.

GRANNY

When Carroll came that winter to buy her land, he found her—at last—ready to sell. The winter was hard and it was time. She had a place to go now that she could stand, and anyway, Preston wasn't paying so much attention to his land but was selling some of it to outsiders now, and hadn't been by in months to chat with her. Without the seasonal rhythms she was used to, Granny was getting bored . . . and she knew what boredom led to at her age. You had to stay shaking, keep moving, never let it rest. Sleep too long . . . you don't wake up. So after demanding—and receiving—a healthy price, she packed up what she figured she would need—two dogs, some chow, some seeds she'd dried the season before, her crocheting supplies, her valuable hand-painted brooch, some clothes, odds and ends, her coffeepot, blackened inside and out from years of coffee made and forgotten, boiling away like her anger, the rocking chair Matthew had carved and made, and some fresh greens Zhena had just brought the day before. And without informing a single other Peavey what she was doing or why or how much she had got for it (and never would, to their very great agitation and consternation), went to live with the only one of her children not certain to drive her crazy with infernal day after day grabbing, buying, wanting, stupidity. Lucille.

They hadn't laid eyes on one another in fifteen years.

CHARLIE CHOW

Charlie Chow built a house that year, one which caused quite a stir; it became in fact one of the more popular topics of conversation in Eunola and a real attraction for visitors to be taken to and shown. Charlie was the town's richest Chinese grocer and the one who had finally broken the color line at the Baptist church downtown (the congregation of which had at first suggested building a separate place of worship for yellow-skinned people out back of the fine brick one), by using his son Charlie, Jr., an outstanding running back on the EHS Hornets, as leverage. Charlie Sr. cashed more white men's checks on Sunday than a bank on Friday. Then he had his own fun playing poker during the week with

Oriental pals, using those Sunday checks as stakes, holding them for weeks at a time as the running game went on, so that if you cashed a check at Charlie Chow's you never knew when it might clear or who might eventually deposit it, worn and brown and fuzzy, creased to fit some wallet or pocket. Well, Charlie saved his money over the years and finally built himself and his family a house, a classic colonial mansion made of fine old dusty-pink bricks, two-storied, with pale green shutters flanking each floor-to-ceiling window and French doors across the back. Sculpted box hedge protected part of the house from view, but people still drove out to see what they could of it, and tell the story. They stopped by the driveway or where the hedge made an arch and watched small almond-colored children play tag in and around fat Doric columns, their perfect Buster Brown haircuts swinging straight, their clothes immaculately clean and starched. When the children ran inside, they slammed a screen door decorated with a wrought-iron nineteenth-century gentleman bowing to a parasoled and hoop-skirted lady. People didn't come by in droves, however, and go home to tell others about it because of how it looked or who lived in it or who was slamming what kind of its front door; they didn't turn the house into a showplace for tourists because of the house itself or even who lived in it. It was its location that lured them . . . where Charlie built. For this great house, which Sexton Cunningham himself would have admired, was situated on the only property in Eunola available to Charlie Chow (except that on the wrong side of Central Avenue which of course Charlie never even considered): behind his store.

SEXTON

Carroll didn't like doing it and neither did the company buying the land—people felt bad enough, he said, about industry moving in, without something like this coming along to make it worse—but it simply didn't make sense to leave it there any more, and so he agreed to handle its removal.

He sold the gates and iron fence for scrap, much to the dismay of a Eunola ladies' club, ordained as keepers of selected historical flames; they said the fence and gates should have been preserved and set up in some suitable place close to downtown for viewing and remembering. But it was too late. Scrap was scrap by the time they heard of it.

He put an ad in the Eunola paper, asking that ancestors of those buried in the old cemetery contact him about exhuming the bodies there. When no one responded he took out another ad and still heard nothing and so, after being told by several reliable advisers that there was no sense digging out there, that most of those people had been buried in wooden caskets which by now would be more than likely rotted away, Carroll went out himself and copied down the names off those small crumbling tombstones and had them all inscribed on one large memorial stone, which was set in their memory and honor in the new cemetery closer to town, the one Lady, Samuel, and Graham were buried in.

Sexton, however, would be moved. So would Corrie Ann. And, of course, Sexton's knight and marble stone.

The day Sexton went was one of those warm ones that

crop up in the middle of winter and send people outside in light sweaters to play ball or golf or putter about in the yard (knowing it's too soon to get serious about anything but maybe some light pruning); when children think spring has come and want to put away their heavy jackets for the year. And so, because of the weather, many Eunolites came out to see. And the extraction, transportation, and relocation of Sexton Cunningham's monument from one graveyard to another became an event even more talked about than the building of Charlie Chow's house, more discussed, in fact, than practically anything.

The cemetery and Granny's property were part of a large tract of land Carroll had sold to the power and light company to build an energy plant on, twenty-two acres in all. It was soon after Granny moved out, that the truck and movers came for Sexton, enabling Granny to brag how close she had come to keeping her promise, when everybody thought all along she was just prattling. She missed staying on her property as long as Sexton was buried there—as she had vowed to—by only a few weeks.

People heard about the move and went out to the old cemetery that warm day, many of them for the first time, to watch as the knight was extracted from its old place beneath the oak, the branches of which had to be cut back in order to lift the statue up with a winch. Sheathed in ropes and chain, the knight was hoisted onto a truck with the marble slab then tied in all directions to the sides of the truck. The people who had come out to see followed it. Wrapped up in thick rope, the statue trembled and nodded as the truck went down the grooved and rutted dirt road past Granny's old house (which still stood, the yard littered with things Peaveys had gone through and decided not to take,

things they left scattered about the yard) to the new cemetery. When others along the way, people who hadn't known
what was happening, spied the truck, they joined the crowd
as well, pulling in behind, until there was a caravan following the knight, while the gravediggers stayed behind to dig
up Sexton's casket and untangle it from the oak's thick roots
and lift it and Corrie Ann's onto another smaller truck to
come along later.

All down the street, as the knight lumbered past, people
stopped to look at it and yell to its parade and even—in the
way people sometimes follow some foolish notion they have
no idea the origin of but follow nonetheless and then giggle
or shrug, wondering what came over them to make them do
something so ridiculous—to wave. As if this were a real live
soldier going by, home victorious from some war, passing
through those who had stayed home and now profited from
his exploits and were showering him with praise.

When the truck arrived, they discovered the main cemetery gates were too low for the knight's head to get through
and had to back up . . . everybody in each car shouting to
the driver of the car directly behind his to BACK UP!
BACK UP! which, the backing up, had to start blocks away
from the cemetery since everybody had stayed bumper to
bumper on the way to town in line behind the big truck.
Then, when he had space enough, the truck driver turned
his rig around and went back down to another entrance—
which he had only just passed a few minutes before—with
no gates, which led to the newer section of the cemetery
where more recently arrived families were buried, where
only thin saplings grew and gravestones were noticeably less
grand. The truck rumbled slowly through that section—
geared down—to the shock and amazement of one ongoing

funeral gathering. They turned to watch the huge gloomy
roped knight nodding in the truck bed, and all his followers,
as they passed through the new section and went on into the
older area, which the front gates opened into, that shadier,
more lush, and better tended section—completely reserved
now—where longer-established Eunola families buried
themselves.

Not all the cars came into the cemetery for the setting up
of the knight. Some only drove along the street and parked
there, feeling it was disrespectful to enter a graveyard simply to gawk. But others not so fearful came on in to watch as
the knight was gradually set up in his new surroundings.
This took quite a while, however, and by the time they were
finished the crowd had thinned considerably, and when the
other, smaller truck arrived with Sexton and Corrie Ann's
caskets (though not the angel, which had been pronounced
irreparable), no one was there to watch. Sexton's body was
lowered into new ground without spectators. At his head
was his dream made tangible. Concrete realization of the
legend he had engendered. Drawing a bead on immortality,
he had bagged it. Independent of time or the shifts of imagination and need it might generate. Susceptible only to the
whim and folly of nature.

The knight became a feature attraction then, which Eunolites brought people to see. And for those who would not
come, out of respect for those buried there, it was an established fact in their minds, this knight standing in their
midst. They were always aware of him, the self-made hero
who never was a soldier and never read a book, who had yet
left behind something outrageous enough to fix his place in
Eunola forever: within the stream of time and outside it.

There were trees in the new cemetery but none as large as

the oak that had once sheltered the knight. The statue now stood between lacy evergreens, which, though lush and well tended, were dwarfed by it, and looked inadequate to guard its great bulk. Now it was unprotected from weather. Soon after it was set in place the warm weather dissipated, a hard freeze gripped the area killing off the grass for a while, and ice closed the knight's gloomy eyes and filled the pocks of his chain mail. Summers, sun poured down on it and made it too hot to touch.

Corrie Ann was on one side of him and on the other, Lady —her grave festooned with Serenthea's dedication and love. Because the monument was so big, it had to be set in front of Sam's grave, and so he was behind them all and set north-south, while they were east-west.

Granny's house was left standing for a while to provide construction workers an office. All her flowers, however, went. Of them, the wisteria died hardest; it had to be hacked at the roots before it gave up and let go.

The power and light company began setting up its generator on the flat, alluvium-rich earth where flowers had once proliferated and cotton was bountiful and the dead were left to themselves; which the ocean and river had over the centuries fortified so generously; where Lolly's baby had been conceived. Superstitious men, the contractor and chief engineer agreed that they could build around it and so the giant oak remained as a totem; a gesture in recognition of the bones beneath it. Then one day coils and cement trucks and pylons appeared; conductors came; cables, grids and poles were set on the flat ground parallel to the solid moss-embellished oak, perpendicular to the earth and sky. Creatures that had once nested in the tree stayed for a while, then, wracked by noise and change, went on. Until only the coils and pylons remained, standing on top of the bones next to the oak. Proudly. As if they'd grown there too.

XIV

LOLLY

The baton inside her skull still turned. She concentrated on its bright residue. Awaiting the baby's birth, looking ahead, she practiced. Sitting very still, honing her craft, she threw the silver stick in lateral twirls as high as treetops, caught it in back bends and splits, wrapped it around her neck and bounced it off her foot, her head high, her teeth sparkling, spectators and fans applauding, the tip-ends of her hair the color of mud overlaid with rust and sunshine grazing her butt. Lolly Ray Lasswell, drenched in light, stared into brightness until brightness was blurred and ran together and filled her eyes even when she closed them. Light bounced off her and, trading reflections with the sun, caused eyes fixed on her to burn, close, and flow. Fire batons illuminated her way. Gold sequins danced about her. The dazzling silver stream, by motion turned into a solid shining disc, marked time just ahead, waiting. She kept all her attention on it, concentrating on it instead of on the fans

around her. Her rapport with time had only been interrupted. If she held to what she had and kept her eyes on the
lodestar, she would find a way to step back into it, she
would. In time.

Hamilton Basso
  The View from Pompey's Head
Richard Bausch
  Real Presence
  Take Me Back
Doris Betts
  The Astronomer and Other Stories
  The Gentle Insurrection and Other
    Stories
Sheila Bosworth
  Almost Innocent
  Slow Poison
David Bottoms
  Easter Weekend
Erskine Caldwell
  Poor Fool
Fred Chappell
  The Gaudy Place
  The Inkling
  It Is Time, Lord
Kelly Cherry
  Augusta Played
Vicki Covington
  Bird of Paradise
Ellen Douglas
  A Family's Affairs
  A Lifetime Burning
  The Rock Cried Out
Percival Everett
  Suder
Peter Feibleman
  The Daughters of Necessity
  A Place Without Twilight
George Garrett
  An Evening Performance
  Do, Lord, Remember Me
Marianne Gingher
  Bobby Rex's Greatest Hit
Shirley Ann Grau
  The House on Coliseum Street
  The Keepers of the House
Barry Hannah
  The Tennis Handsome
Donald Hays
  The Dixie Association

William Humphrey
  Home from the Hill
  The Ordways
Mac Hyman
  No Time For Sergeants
Madison Jones
  A Cry of Absence
Nancy Lemann
  Lives of the Saints
  Sportsman's Paradise
Beverly Lowry
  Come Back, Lolly Ray
Willie Morris
  The Last of the Southern Girls
Louis D. Rubin, Jr.
  The Golden Weather
Evelyn Scott
  The Wave
Lee Smith
  The Last Day the Dogbushes Bloomed
Elizabeth Spencer
  The Salt Line
  This Crooked Way
  The Voice at the Back Door
Max Steele
  Debby
Walter Sullivan
  The Long, Long Love
Allen Tate
  The Fathers
Peter Taylor
  The Widows of Thornton
Robert Penn Warren
  Band of Angels
  Brother to Dragons
  World Enough and Time
Walter White
  Flight
James Wilcox
  North Gladiola
Joan Williams
  The Morning and the Evening
  The Wintering
Thomas Wolfe
  The Hills Beyond
  The Web and the Rock